Aria

Happily After When

A 12 book series, inspired by fairytales and the ugliness of real life.
Books are sequential, and highly recommended to be read in publication
order.

Jazz
An Aladdin retelling

Aria
A Little Mermaid Retelling

Cara
A Cinderella Retelling

Sachi
A Snow White Retelling

And more to follow...

HAPPILY AFTER WHEN BOOK 1

when envy has a weapon

Aria

EMILY BOURNE

First Published by Halo & Claws Publishing 2020

ARIA

Happily After When - Book 2

Copyright © Emily Bourne 2020

For information contact: https://www.hcpbooks.com

Stock Images via Bigstock, Shutterstock

ISBN: 978-1-925990-08-9

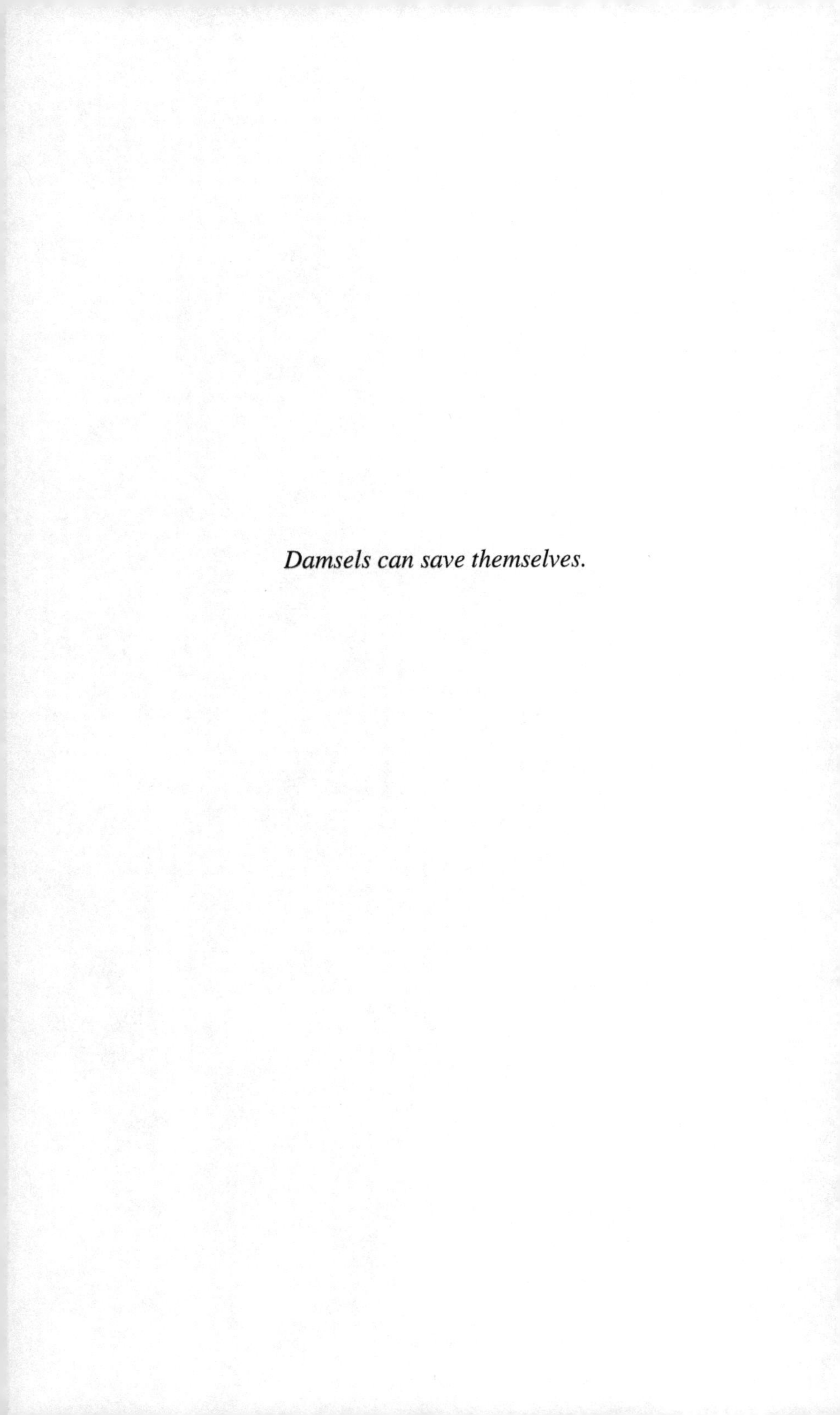

Damsels can save themselves.

Celebrate

Aria follows her family into St Paolo's Restaurant. It's one of the finest restaurants in the dining precinct between Province and the Business District. It has the traditional red and white checkerboard tablecloths, chunky white candle centrepieces, and the perpetual smell of pepperoni, meatballs, and parmesan cheese. It's a place that should be out of her parents' price range, but they deemed this celebration the most special of occasions.

Pride shimmers in her father's eyes as the hostess shows the family to their reserved table.

"Bottle of champagne," her father, Angelo, orders as they take their seats. "We are here to celebrate my daughter Aria's great achievement."

Aria smiles, glad to see her parents' happiness, yet she is very aware of her seething sister beside her. She can't decide which fear is greater. Not fulfilling her parents' wildest dreams or making her sister Valeria angry. And she didn't know how to do one without doing the other.

When champagne fills their glasses, Aria notices the tears welling in her mother's eyes. "You ok, Ma?" she asks.

Her mother smiles and nods. "Very."

"To Nationals!" Angelo cheers, raising his bubbling champagne glass.

All four glasses meet in the middle of the table.

Clink.

"Yes, Aria," Valeria says, after a sip of champagne. "You've got a lot of work ahead of you."

"As you should have," Angelo remarks.

Irritation drags Valeria's frown downward. Her eyes narrow and her glare intensifies at Aria.

Aria sets her champagne glass down and shifts on her seat. She clears her throat and then says, "I hope I don't disappoint you all."

"We'll work hard," Angelo says and takes another sip of champagne. "With my coaching, you will win the championship." His eyes move to Valeria. "We won't fail."

Valeria's jaw rocks, and when she moves on her seat, Aria flinches in reaction.

"Jumpy, Aria?" Valeria asks, mockingly.

Aria picks up a menu, but her trembling fingers betray her.

A whisper of laughter escapes her sister.

"Angelo Rivera!" a voice booms from the entrance of the restaurant.

The family turns to the voice and finds Angelo's brother and his family. Angelo's body tightens, and a scowl twists his expression.

"Long time no see," Aria's Uncle Franco says, stepping their way.

Aria looks past him to see her cousins, especially Helen. It has been years since they last saw one another. Aria gets a flash of the pair in the church choir robes they would wear every Sunday. She musters enough courage to wave at Helen.

"You can't find another restaurant to go to?" Angelo says with a clenched jaw.

Franco's arms shoot out wide. "We come here every Saturday

night. We never see you here. I assumed you couldn't afford it."

"I can afford more than you think," Angelo grumbles.

"Since when?" Franco asks with a jovial laugh. He crosses his arms and sends a smirk to his wife. "You still being a wimp, Angelo? Shutting your family away from the public?"

"No concern of yours," Angelo says, picking up a menu and shifting in his seat.

"Johnny and Lou will be here soon with their families," Franco says. "Please, come to your senses and re-join the family. This so-called feud is silly."

Angelo stands, throwing his napkin over his place-setting. "To you, maybe."

Aria's stomach cramps. She knows her father's actions well and doesn't like where this encounter is going.

"Don't be like this, Angelo," Franco says with a sour frown. "No one cares about how poor you are or how much time you waste by the edge of the swimming pool. You don't have to shut yourself off just because—"

"—Let's go," Angelo barks at his family. He lifts his arm up with force. "Up! Now!"

Aria, her mother and sister get up from their seats and promptly follow Angelo away from the table.

Franco's arms swing out wide and his mouth hangs open. "Please. Come on."

Angelo flicks a hand Franco's way, avoiding eye contact as he marches towards the restaurant's front door.

"You're being ridiculous," Franco calls out as the family exits onto the sidewalk.

Angelo grabs Aria's wrist, pulling her uncomfortably close. "You will win the Championship. Don't you dare make me look like a fool."

Aria's shoulders bunch high as she cowers beneath his heaving frame. "Yes, Pappa."

Angelo lets her go, tossing her arm with frustration.

"Nice going," Valeria snides, nudging Aria's arm as she brushes past.

Valeria's right eyebrow arches high as she follows her father to the car, keeping her stare on Aria. Enjoyment curls her lips.

Aria looks back to the restaurant. Helen gives her a defeated smile and a limp wave goodbye.

At home, Aria escapes into the shower. She turns the water as hot as it will go. Hot water is a rare nicety. She closes her eyes and the water cascades over her hair. Aria takes a half step back, so the water hits her face. For a moment, she holds her breath and takes in the sound of her heartbeat.

Slow and low.

Happiness is another rare nicety. When was the last time she felt that? She remembers it feeling similar to hot water, and that makes her smile. Seeing Helen reminds her of happiness. Reminds her of singing.

A hymn from church plays at her tongue, and she lets the melodic lyrics glide from her throat and echo in the shower. Her heart flutters at the freedom in making music with her voice and she opens her eyes.

The song stays in her head as she dresses and then disappears as she makes her way up the hall to her bedroom.

Aria sits at her dresser and glides her hairbrush through her damp auburn hair. She watches herself in the dresser mirror. Her strokes are gradual and gentle. Brushing her hair is the closest to peace she feels. A moment just for her.

Valeria bursts into their twin bedroom and pounces on her bed. "You really screwed up tonight, Aria."

Aria continues with her brush strokes, watching her sister from the corner of her eye. "Aren't you going to say your prayers before laying on your bed?"

Valeria groans and pulls herself off the bed.

Valeria kneels beside her bed, clasping her hands in front of her face. "Dear God, please watch over my family…" Aria tenses every time her sister tells her prayers aloud. It always sounds like prayers that God would look unkindly on. "…and especially look out for my little sister, Aria. She has so much work to do. So much pressure on her shoulders. Hopefully, the pressure doesn't hold her under water too long."

"*Valeria*," Aria whispers.

"Amen," Valeria says, and makes the sign of the cross. She flicks her eyes to Aria with a devious smile. "What? You know you shouldn't interrupt someone in the middle of prayer."

"You shouldn't say such mean-spirited things to God."

"It wasn't. I genuinely hope the pressure doesn't drown you."

Chills race down Aria's spine. Her jaw clenches and her trembling forces her to drop the hairbrush on the dresser.

"Say your prayers, dear sister," Valeria says, pulling back the covers on her bed.

Their bedroom is small and narrow. Their shared dresser and compact wardrobe crowd the space near the door. Their single beds fit snuggly against the walls with space for one person to kneel between them. The walls are cloud grey, and a picture frame hangs over each bed. An image depicting the Madonna hangs over Valeria's bed, and an image of Christ hangs over Aria's bed. A small window sits between the beds, and even though it's only working-class Hamlet outside, the view is the most interesting thing about the bedroom.

Aria moves to her bed and views pieces of broken scissors between the sheets of Valeria's bed. "Why do you have that in your bed?"

Valeria winks. "I'm making you a present."

Aria shivers as she turns her back on her sister and kneels by her bed. She makes the sign of the cross and clasps her hands. She takes in a deep breath and closes her eyes.

Dear God, is life supposed to be this hard? I'm eighteen. Am I supposed to decide things for myself now? Or do I have to wait until I'm married and out from under this roof?

Please, God, help Pappa. He is so mad. Is it because he's sad? His whole life is a fight with his brothers. If I don't win Nationals, he'll never forgive me. Please, help me be strong. I need to win for him. And Mamma.

Please, watch over Valeria. She is mad too. She is mad at me. She blames me for beating her at the State Championships. She blames me for her not placing. Please, help her cope. I know she's a good person. There is a good person in my sister. She is just lost. I can help her. Please, show me how to help her.

Amen.

Aria opens her eyes and slides onto her bed.

"Did you ask God to take you in your sleep?" Valeria asks, twirling a jagged blade between her fingers.

Aria's body is so tense she might snap in half. "What?"

"You know," Valeria replies, reclining on her bed. "*If I die before I wake…*"

"Oh. No, I didn't say that prayer."

"But what happens when you die in your sleep?"

"When?"

"Everyone dies one day, dear sister."

"I'm tired," Aria says, flicking off the lamp between their beds. "Good night, Valeria."

Valeria snickers to herself. "Ok. Good night."

Aria pulls the covers to her chin. Darkness consumes the room, yet her eyes seem glued open. Her mind rewinds to her last choir practice. It was four years ago, but seeing Helen tonight makes the memory feel like yesterday.

Reminiscing is too painful.

Aria's jolts out of her thoughts by the sounds of a blade sharpening. She looks to her side and springs to sitting. The dark outline of her sister sits on her bed, clinking broken pieces of metal together.

"*Valeria*," Aria hisses, a hand resting on her terrorised heart.

"What? Were you sleeping?" Valeria asks with a hint of glee.

Aria's falls back to the mattress, confused by her sister's words.

With agility, Valeria launches off her bed, a blade directed at Aria.

Aria pushes towards the wall; a scream rushing out her.

Valeria shooshes her, running a blade delicately over Aria's cheek.

"Don't wake Ma and Pappa," Valeria warns in a whisper. "Then you'll really be in trouble."

Valeria moves back to her bed, flinging the piece of metal towards Aria's bed.

Aria squeaks in fright, flinging the ridged metal off her wrist. The serrated edge nicks her skin. The scratch is hot, and she puts pressure on the area. It oozes slightly, but not bad enough for a bandage.

Why is she always taking these things from Pa's tool shed? She collects these items and only does wicked things with them.

Aria lets out a weighted breath and looks to her sister's bed. A shadowy lump curls up on the bed.

She lies down, feeling more awake than ever. *Not the first night without sleep.* She eyes her sister's blanketed body and feels a new level of rigid. She will stay this tense until she hears sleep noises from Valeria. And even then, any sleep she gets will be broken by her self-inflicted nightmares.

Dream

Aria glides through the water the next day, her limbs strong and purposeful. Her breaths above the water are quick, careful to not take in any of her father's drill-sergeant commands from the swimming pool's edge.

She wills her body not to give into the exhaustion already plaguing her mind from another sleepless night. How could she possibly sleep when it's impossible to know if and when her sister would strike her?

Her moves are robotic, but she's certain she's making a personal-best. As she tumbles at the pool's end for her next lap, she wonders whether she should care more. She'll shave another minute off her PB. But what did it really mean? Why did she get so much praise for swimming in a lap pool?

She takes a breather after twenty laps and rests her back against the tiles. She listens to the noise of the water as she swirls her legs beneath the surface. Her eyes wander around the other lanes and stop when a pair of green eyes look back at her.

The eyes belong to a striking young man with classically handsome features and side swept blonde hair. Aria has noticed him before. She knows she should think about her swimming technique and worries if Pa will snap at her for resting, but she can't keep her eyes off him.

There's something wonderful about him.

His rosy lips spread into a smile. A smile aimed at her. He lifts his hand and gives her a wave.

Her heart flutters into overdrive. Her blood pumps faster than any record-breaking lap could ever get it to do.

She smiles back. *He's waving at me?*

Before she can lift her hand, her father's voice commands her from the pool's edge. "Aria! Another ten laps. Get moving!"

Aria is quick to launch into another lap. She doesn't want her father embarrassing her in the water.

After finishing her last ten laps, Aria pulls herself up and out of the water.

"Great time, Aria," her father cheers, raising his stopwatch in the air.

Aria draws a limp smile, pretending to note the time displayed.

Her father roughly pats her shoulder, saying loud enough for all the swimming pool patrons to hear, "The new National Champion is right here."

Aria slouches her shoulders and wrings out her soaked auburn hair. The National Championships are two months away, and she doesn't appreciate the mounds of pressure he adds every day.

"You look sluggish," her father says, frowning as he looks at her sideways. "We need to up your protein intake."

She waves him off, moving toward her towel. "I'm fine. It's just the extra laps you made me do."

"*Rubbish*," her father dismisses. "You were making great time and could have gotten in a few more laps."

Aria shuts her eyes tight and dries her face. *Fine. Why do I bother trying to share my feelings?*

"Just because you won the State Championships doesn't mean you can get complacent," her father says, looming behind her. "You need to train even harder now and stick to this stricter regime."

Aria shakes off the chill in the air and wraps the towel around her body. "Yes, Pappa, I know."

Aria spies her sister pulling herself out of the water and removing the cap from her head. As Valeria's chocolaty hair sweeps over and below her shoulders, her steely hazel eyes deadpan at Aria. Aria notes the pang in her chest and pulls at the towel across her shoulders, turning toward the female changing rooms.

"Remember, you represent the family," Angelo says gruffly, before she walks away. "You keep up your training. You will not make me a laughingstock. Maiden City needs to see I'm the best coach in the area. You represent my methods. Remember that."

Aria avoids her father's eyes and nods. She makes her way to the changing rooms, dread seeping from her stomach to her heart. *Make him a success, that's all I'm worth.*

Their family lives in Hamlet, the working-class area of Maiden City. However, with her father dedicating all his time to her swimming training, and her mother not working, their lack of money coming in could force them into The Limits. She needs to win the Championships. The Championship leads to sponsorships and prize money.

Her father gave up his landscaping and pool cleaning work to train her and her sister full-time. If she doesn't bring money into the family, she'll never forgive herself.

The public swimming pool desperately needs funding, like everything in Maiden City below the Business District. Sometimes she dreams about a sponsorship from Ultimate ME Fitness Group. She trained in one of their gyms after she won a local swim-meet. It was a promotional thing for the gym, but she loved using the fancy equipment and swimming in their sparkling lap pool. Maybe swimming every day wouldn't be that bad if she could be in a place like that.

In the changing room, Aria tries to pull her father's orders from her head. He relentlessly drilled her about her technique today.

Seeing his brother has really rattled him. He's so much worse lately. Especially after Uncle Franco's comment about his family regularly dining at St Paolo's. If we had eaten there, it could have meant Pappa not being able to pay a utility bill.

Aria leaves her shower stall and sheepishly approaches her sister. She clears her throat to gain Valeria's attention.

Valeria cracks her neck. "What?"

Aria jumps a half step back. "Um, I was wondering if... um, now that Pa said... that, um..."

"Spit it out, moron."

"Are you gonna start dating?" Aria blurts.

Valeria cackles, shoving her towel and swimwear into her bag. "Why are you asking me such stupid questions?"

Aria's shoulders droop.

Valeria nudges Aria, making her almost lose balance. "Why are you asking about dating?"

"Well, Pa said you could," Aria whispers. "And... and I can't until..."

Valeria's eyes slit at Aria. "You want to start dating?"

Aria shrugs. "It could be nice?"

"Like you'd swap places with me if it meant you could date?"

"The idea of dating makes me happier than the thought of winning the Championship. When I think about the competition, all I feel is dread." Aria takes a deep breath in and out. "I would swap places with you, if I could."

Valeria runs a hand through her hair, eyes drifting upwards in thought. "If that's what you really want, you should tell Pa."

"Really?"

"Why would he stop you from pursuing your dreams?" Valeria replies, a softness to her voice. "Does dating sound like a dream?"

Aria nods and whispers, "Yes."

Valeria points to the entrance. "Then go. Go tell Pa now. Don't wait and lose your nerve. Ask him to meet the boy you want to date."

Aria hugs her middle. "Here? Now?"

"Go," Valeria urges, pushing her towards the door.

Aria trips her way outside, and keeps the speed Valeria started her on, even though Valeria didn't continue behind her.

"Um, Pa," Aria begins.

Her father scrutinises her. "Are you ready to go? Where's your bag?"

"With Valeria. Speaking of Valeria, you said she could date," Aria says, her insides contorting. "I'm eighteen and thought that might mean I could—"

"—No dating!" he spits the words. He looms over Aria. "I could not have been clearer about that. Not when you're training for the Championship. You are to focus on your training. That's final."

Aria shivers under his roaring tirade. "Ok. Yes, Pa."

She looks behind her to see her sister giggling to herself in the entrance of the changing room.

"Go inside and get your sister," Angelo says. "And remind *her* to find a boy to date. I want her married off and out of my house."

As Aria turns to the changing room, she can still make out her sister. The sting of her father's comment showing in the scowl on her face.

Refreshed

Eddy's head bobs in and out of the water as he tries his best to clear his mind. He helps many clients with meditation practices and had decided it was time to take his own advice. Before going into the refuge centre for work, he now starts his day going to Maiden City Swimming Pool to get in a few laps and centre his mind.

Eddy never truly turns off. He's shy of twenty-two-years-old, but his stress levels make him feel older than his years. His mind drifts over his last therapy session, from the day before, with young Max.

"What do you think you'd do if you saw your brother today?" Eddy asked Max as they wrapped up their counselling session.

"I think I'd turn and run," Max said, flexing his hand in and out of a fist.

Eddy's eyes widened, and a smile lifted his face. "That's a massive improvement. You're not going straight to violence. Maxy, I'm so proud of you."

Max grinned, standing from the couch and turning to the door. "You're a cool dude, Ed. Thanks for the chat."

Eddy lifted a hand in a wave. "Anytime, mate."

Even remembering last night's events makes him exhausted. With the family Max came from, Eddy is always sure to take special care of him. He doesn't want to trip up and make another mistake like he did with DJ. But the workload has never felt this exhausting.

Jazz Abadi means well with all her marketing efforts to get the shelter known in the community, so those who need help know where to go. But since she's helped run the shelter, things have gone from zero-to-one-hundred. Eddy hasn't been able to turn off in weeks. The stories, tragedies, and abuse he's told about plague him and he doesn't know how many more days he can go on with next-to-no sleep.

The water struggles to keep him calm. His heart palpitates in his chest. With every trick he knows, he tries to switch off his brain. He slows his pace in the water and eyes the side of the pool. *Maybe the red-haired girl will be here?*

His head clears with just the thought of her. Yesterday they made eye contact, and he could swear she was going to wave back to him.

It can be so hard to make out who is who when everyone is in swimming lanes. He often has to wait until he's done for the day to see if she's here.

Whenever he makes it to the pool at the same time she does, it lifts his spirits. He's never spoken to her or gotten close to her, but there's something about her. Her graceful yet powerful movements in the water. The way she seems to be in her own thoughts when she walks away from the pool.

Eddy wants to know more about her. To have a conversation with her. To ask her out for coffee or dinner.

He laughs to himself. *As if I have any free time for dating.*

Noise fills his head again. He presses on in his swimming lane.

Under the water, he takes in the quiet serenity. He concentrates on steady breathing to release his anxiety. He drowns out the mess of busy thoughts and is present with his breath. He pushes through the water with extra strength.

Several laps later, he feels better. Renewed and refreshed, he pulls himself out of the pool and walks to his towel. He wraps it around his waist and notices two girls walking away from the pool. One pulls off her swimming cap and hair, the colour of a crackling fire, cascades down her back.

It's her.

Joy fills his soul and his heart thumps against his chest. He tries to think of a good opening line as the girls walk towards their coach.

He yells at the girls as they approach.

That's no way for a coach to talk to people.

"That's the Rivera family," a man at the kiosk says as Eddy passes. "The youngest daughter just won the State Championship. Freestyle fifty, one-hundred, and two-hundred metres. Angelo sure got a lot to prove right now."

"That's all he does now," says a man leaning against the kiosk. "Trains his girls to be champs. No wonder he's stressed out."

Eddy notes the slumped and subservient demeanours of the girls. Sisters. His stomach clamps, all too aware of the signs of domestic abuse.

Unable to turn off, he keeps eyes on the girls. The brunette sister watches the red-haired sister, whose eyes are adrift. Her body is present, but her mind is not.

Eddy had just thought how adorable that look had been, but now it made him sad. Knots reshape in his back. It would be wrong not to keep eyes on the family. He hopes beyond hope he's wrong, but with everything he's seen and heard over the past few years, he doubts it.

He eyes the father yelling at the girls and his fists tightened.

The girls are dismissed to the changing rooms, and Eddy watches the father make his way to a bench.

So much for feeling refreshed. He moves to the changing room to take a shower and hopes for at least a minute of peace before going into work.

After his shower, he leaves the changing room with eyes peeled for the girls' father. He wants to see how he acts when they aren't around.

He moves along the cement path, and stops by a wall of the female changing room. He looks up to a vent where the most angelic singing voice filters through.

He drops his bag at the same time his mouth falls open.

Wow.

Goosebumps sprout on his limbs, and a tingle runs down his spine.

The voice morphs into a beautiful hum and moves to the entrance of the changing room. The sunlight grows warmer as it shines on the alluring flame red hair of the girl who calms his thoughts.

Her hazel eyes meet his, and she grows mute. The blush of her cheeks highlights her freckles, making her even more adorable.

His smile hurts his cheeks, and all he can think to say is, "Hi. Was that you singing?"

She purses her lips in a timid smile and gives a slight nod.

He takes a step forward. "Wow. You have an incredible voice."

She stares at him. Frozen.

Eddy takes a step back, unable to work out if she is acting well or badly to him.

His eyes narrow with concern. He asks softly, "Are you ok?"

"Move it!" a voice yells.

Her sister marches out of the change room, pushing her forward.

"C'mon," the sister orders. "Pa's waiting."

Eddy tries to grab their attention, but they speed towards their father, who is already walking towards the exit.

Eddy tenses, wanting to find out where the family is going and to make sure the girls are ok. But work is calling him.

Work is always calling him.

Foolish

Aria skips up the hall. Electricity tingles under her skin. The blonde boy that smiled at her won't leave her head. Her heart flutters and she dares a smile.

He said I have a nice singing voice.

She walks the hall to her bedroom, her head in the clouds and a song at her lips. "*We shall reach the summer land, Some sweet day, by and—*"

A scream breaks out behind her. The wind knocks out of her, and she spins around to see her mother at the end of the hall.

Her mother's mouth hangs open, her cheeks sunken and eyes circular in shocked disgust. "Shut your mouth!" her mother bellows.

Aria dips her head and her shoulders bunch high. Her back curves and she scuffs the floor. "Sorry, Mamma."

Her heart throbs in her chest. Filled with stupidity and guilt, she retreats to her bedroom.

Don't try to be happy, she reminds herself. She closes her eyes and focuses on swimming techniques. *That's all you're allowed to think about.*

Aria presses her hands into her stomach, taking long breaths in and out. The weight on her shoulders enforces the pressure on her. She needs to win Nationals for her parents. The sacrifices will be worth it to fulfil their wishes. They already gave up so much to make her a winner.

"Being stupid again, princess?" Valeria taunts, barging her way into their bedroom.

"No," Aria replies, almost inaudible.

Valeria slides onto her bed and narrows her eyes at Aria. "You made a whole heap of foolish mistakes today."

Aria grabs her hairbrush and turns her back on her sister. "I swam one-hundred laps today."

Valeria scoffs a laugh. "That's not what I'm talking about."

Aria brushes her auburn hair as knots tie along her spine.

"I saw the way you were eyeing that boy," Valeria says.

"He talked to me," Aria is quick to deflect, "I didn't talk to him."

"What if Pa saw?"

Aria frowns. "I know."

Valeria perches on her bed, an excited bounce to her legs. "It doesn't have to be like this, you know."

"What do you mean?"

"You could run away."

Aria gasps. "Don't say such things."

"Don't you want to be happy?"

"I want to be with my family."

"You don't want a boyfriend? A husband?"

Aria's stomach flips. The idea of these things makes her heart swell, but pursuing them over her family's needs fills her with guilt.

"Don't you?" Aria asks.

"We're not talking about me," Valeria says. "I have options. What about you? What are you going to do about it?"

"Nothing. There's nothing I can do." *Unless I fail in the water like her.* "You won't tell Pa about the boy, will you?"

Valeria smirks. "And where would the fun in that be?"

Aria sucks in a breath and turns away from her sister.

"But that's not the stupidest thing you did today."

Aria closes her eyes, wanting nothing more than to drown out her sister's words.

"You make things one-hundred times worse by opening your mouth."

Aria's stomach swishes. "I didn't talk to him."

"You sang, you idiot. In front of Mamma."

Aria rolls her shoulders in circles and stretches her neck, straining under the mounting pressure. "I didn't mean to. It just slipped out. I wasn't thinking."

"Maybe you would've been better off if God gave you a brain instead of arms and legs to swim with," Valeria hits back. "You are such a moron."

Aria places the hairbrush down and draws out a breath. She closes her eyes and her body sways. *Your words can't hurt me. Your words can't hurt me. Your words can't hurt me.* She inhales quickly. *God save me.*

Grateful

Valeria fluffs her hair at the mirror and then runs a finger below her winged eyeliner. "Don't miss me too much, dear sister."

"Since when are you going out on a date?" Aria asks.

Valeria smiles at her reflection. *It's so easy to get under her skin.*

"You didn't think he was interested in you, did you?"

Shock covers Aria's face.

Too easy.

Aria hugs her middle and looks down to the floor. "What? No. Of course not. I don't know who you are going on a date with."

Valeria finishes a layer of lipstick and blows a kiss at Aria's reflection. "Don't worry your pretty little head about it. I'll show him a good time."

Valeria watches Aria shudder from the corner of her eye.

"Do nothing stupid while I'm gone."

"Like what?"

Valeria laughs. "True. Anything you do would be stupid. All you know is swimming. With everything else, you're a grade-A moron."

"I'm not allowed to do anything else," Aria mutters.

Valeria moves away from the dresser and saunters over to Aria's bed. "You could go in my place."

"Huh?"

"Go on the date instead of me. He's waiting for you. You'd be happy."

Aria's eyes zigzag in confusion. "I can't do that."

"Show him a good time. You know you want to."

Aria hesitates. She utters noises, but no words.

Valeria groans, sick of Aria's non-commitment to anything non-swimming. Without a moment's thought, she lunges at Aria and grabs her neck. She squeezes her throat and smiles at the way Aria gasps for air.

"This is your punishment," Valeria whispers as Aria struggles against her. "You get to sit in this room all night, while I go out with the boy you've been staring at all week. Enjoy thinking about my lips on his."

Valeria lets go of her sister, flinging her backwards on the bed. She whips around to the door, leaves the room, slamming the door behind her.

She rests against the door, a soft giggle slipping out of her. *I hope she's crying in there.*

Valeria smooths down her knee-length black dress and moves towards the living room.

"Is Tony here yet?" she asks her parents, who sit on a sofa together.

"Not yet," her father says. "I'm so happy you are finally going on a date with him."

"You might miss me when I'm out of the house," Valeria replies.

"You need to be making your own house," her mother says.

Valeria's mood sours. She crosses her arms and slouches.

"Stand up straight," her father orders as he gets off the couch. "Be a lady."

Aria had told her she'd swap places with her if it meant she could date. But she's too chicken to do it. It makes Valeria's blood boil that Aria is so flippant with her swimming talent. Why is Aria so blessed when Valeria is hungrier for the accolades? *Doesn't she understand how lucky she is?*

When Valeria worked out which boy Aria is lusting over, she couldn't help tormenting her. It is too easy to make Aria believe he is the boy courting her.

Getting a last-minute date for tonight was easy. Tony Moretti had already asked her on several dates, but she's always denied him because she puts swimming training first.

No late nights.

Her parents know Tony and his family, so getting them to agree was a piece of cake. Her father often spoke about wanting Valeria married, so he approved the date instantly.

Part of her wishes she'd just faked the date. But she wouldn't keep herself out of her father's sight for long enough, so she lets Tony take her on a real date.

Ick.

"Tony!" her father cheers, opening the front door.

"Hi Mr Rivera," Tony says, holding a bunch of white lilies. "Is Valeria ready?"

"I'm here," Valeria says, strutting towards the front door. "Don't wait up, Pa."

"You'll be home by ten."

Valeria shrugs, linking her arm with Tony's. "We'll see." She grabs the bouquet from Tony. "Thanks." She chucks them inside the house. "Tell Ma to put them in some water, would ya."

She closes the door on her father and pulls Tony towards his car.

"*Whoah*, you speak to your father like that?" Tony asks, alarmed.

"If you want to make a lasting impression, you gotta go big. He's gonna wish he never let me out of the house with you."

"I was surprised your father agreed to us seeing each other," Tony tells. "When he made that big stink about your family not socialising with anyone from church, I didn't know how he would react."

"My father only thinks he wants me out of the house. I'll make him see the light."

"We can have fun tonight," Tony says with a dopey grin. "You were so fun when we were kids. So adventurous, and the best at playing house."

"Playing is all we are doing tonight. Get it through your thick head. This is not a real date."

Tony gulps. "Wait. You don't wanna go on this date with me?"

Valeria groans and rolls her eyes. "Boy, can you try to play along. Just make sure I break curfew, ok?"

"Your father knows my father. I don't want it going around the neighbourhood I'm a—"

"—Tony! Can't you do one thing for me? I thought you were supposed to like me?"

Tony's eyes shine as he looks into hers. "I do like you. You're so pretty."

"Don't make me barf."

"I'm sorry?"

"And, by the way, I hate flowers," she says, getting into his car.

"Oh."

"Now drive, boy."

Tony buckles his seatbelt and says, "There's this really nice bar in the Nightclub District that does—"

"—Gross. Pa will hate it. Let's go."

"Do you want to hear more about it?"

"For goodness' sake, Tony. I'm not going on this date to talk. Let's go."

"I don't remember you being this aggressive," Tony murmurs.

"I have a plan, Tony. Be grateful you're helping me with it."

Happy

Aria coughs so violently that every spring in the mattress pushes against her body. She lifts herself up and rubs her swollen neck.

No blood.

Valeria didn't dig in her fingernails this time.

She's always shared a room with Valeria, and they've never been friends. Valeria is two years older and acts like the age gap is bigger. Her belittlement of Aria worsening throughout their teenage years.

Aria wishes their father paid more attention to Valeria. She's tried to get him to focus on Valeria's abilities, but when she didn't place at the State Championships, Angelo really ignored her. It pains Aria, but more so, it scares her. She knows how easily her sister can become unhinged. Especially when most of her attacks come out of nowhere.

Aria never dreamt her words could have so much impact. That mentioning dating would lead to Valeria going out on a date.

Valeria's going out with the boy I like? Aria's stomach churns. *Is that why she pulled me away from him so fast? To have him to herself?*

Aria makes her way out of the bedroom for dinner with her parents. White petals lay on the worn carpet. She scoops them up and hears her mother in the kitchen.

"What are these from?" she asks, holding the petals as she approaches her mother.

Her mother lifts a vase away from the sink and places it on the bench. "Tony Moretti brought his bouquet for Valeria. The ungrateful little girl chucked them on the floor."

Aria looks at the vase of lilies and smiles. "Tony Moretti?"

"Yes. Valeria's date."

Butterflies fill Aria's stomach and her smile spreads.

Her mother *tsks*. "I pray that boy can stand her attitude. She needs to zip that lip for him to propose."

Aria walks to the vase and takes a whiff of their sweet perfume. "Do you think Valeria wants to get married?"

"What is this *want*?" her mother snaps. "She will get married. That's what we do."

"Even me?"

"Don't be stupid, Aria." Her mother walks out of the kitchen. "You focus on swimming. When you retire, we will find you someone."

It will never be enough. She will train her hardest to win the National Championships, but it won't be enough for her parents to let her make her own decisions. To let her go. To let her be her own person.

Will winning a World Championship and gaining a World Record be enough?

She walks to the dining table but doesn't sit.

"I'm not hungry," she says. "I'm going to bed."

"Nonsense," her father says, slamming a fist on the table. "Sit and eat. You don't become Champion by skipping meals. You need to stick to my regime. Remember?"

Aria frowns and slides back a chair. "Yes, Pa."

"You can't fail me," he tells her. "You keep winning, and then we can bring other things back into our lives. Until then, we need to focus, one-hundred percent."

Aria sits and eats her meal. She doesn't taste it. Her mind is elsewhere. To the flowers. To those bewitching green eyes.

The tension inside her body dissipates as that handsome boy fills her mind. She imagines him at her doorstep, bringing her flowers. She imagines him taking her to dinner at St Paolo's.

They would be seated at a table and her aunts, uncles, and cousins would greet them. They wouldn't have to run out, they'd all be friendly. The wait staff would move all the tables into one long-stretched table. All the extended family would join them.

Aria sighs. They used to have big family gatherings with food up to their eyeballs. That was taken away too.

Shut away from everyone to make one man happy.

She stares at her father as he eats.

Is he happy yet?

After dinner, Aria sits in her bedroom, staring at the adjacent bed. With Valeria gone, she considers this an opportunity to catch a few hours of needed sleep.

It still wouldn't be restful.

Aria knows her sister well. The date could be a ploy to get Aria to relax, and then her sister would jump out and attack her.

Her eyes wander along the coverings of Valeria's bed. *Could I get rid of all the nasty stuff she's hiding in there? Is it all in her sheets, or under the mattress too?*

She quickly quashes the thoughts.

It'll hurt more if she knows I messed with her stuff.

Aria shudders. Even when she's not in the room, Valeria's threats still linger.

She lies down on her bed, lights out, and stares at the ceiling. Aria would do anything to give away swimming. If she could, she'd give every ounce of her talent to her sister.

She would love to go back to school. She'd love to learn about history, art, math, or science. Anything other than swimming all day, every day.

The thoughts lull her into a light sleep. Her breaths are shallow, and her chest rises and falls with an easy rhythm.

"BOO!"

Aria leaps out of sleep. She sits in her bed, darkness surrounding her, and the quiet laughter of her sister moving towards her bed.

"Just wanted to let you know I'm back home," Valeria whispers from her bed.

Aria's hand plants on her racing heart. Through laboured breaths, she asks, "What time is it?"

"Close to midnight."

"Pa let you stay out that late?"

"Nope. I broke curfew."

Aria slides down on her bed, slick with sweat. *Should have known Valeria was out to start trouble.*

Aria's eyes stay open for the rest of the night. They are crusty and raw as day breaks. She pulls herself out of bed and gets ready for swimming training.

Valeria soundly sleeps in her bed.

Odd.

Valeria is always up promptly for swimming training.

Aria doesn't want to touch her, for fear it's a trick. However, if Valeria is sleeping, she doesn't want her father scolding her for not getting up.

She lightly taps her.

Nothing.

"Valeria," she whispers, nudging her a little harder.

Valeria groans and swats at Aria.

"We need to get going," Aria whispers.

Valeria grumbles more sounds and flips over in the bed, pulling her comforter over her head.

"C'mon. Pa will want to go soon."

Valeria doesn't budge.

Aria grabs her bag and makes her way out of the bedroom.

Here goes nothing.

She meets her father in the living room.

"Ready to go?" he asks.

"Valeria's not up," she says, like she's confessing to a crime.

"*Pfft*. What does it matter? Get in the car."

"Won't you wake her up?"

"In the car, Aria," he orders, pushing her towards the door.

Invisible

Valeria is annoyed her father didn't come in and order her out of bed. But she prepared for that.

When she gets to training late, he will really lose it. *He will be so mad when I embarrass him in public. It will force him to pay attention to me.*

She was awake before her sister got out of bed, but she needed to put on a show. Now that she's alone in the bedroom, Valeria pulls down the bed cover and gags on last night's memories.

A glitzy bar in the Nightclub District with an atrocious open mic night. Tony asked her if she was having fun, and she replied that if she wanted to listen to cats being strangled, she could have gone to the alley behind her house. That part makes her smile because it made Tony shut up for the rest of the evening.

Pa is angry at me for not placing at the State Championships. He wants to marry me off as punishment. Make me somebody else's problem. But I'll get my place at Nationals, and then he'll ban me from dating again. I can stay home forever.

Last night she grabbed a hold of Tony like a vice grip and dragged him to her front door. She wouldn't let him leave until her father opened the door. Then she laid the biggest kiss of her life on his lips.

Remembering the kiss made her grimace. *Wet, sloppy, ugh, not worth it.* She had better kisses when she attended Catholic school.

Her father snapped at her to get inside the house, like she wanted, but he didn't continue to yell at her. He just told Tony to go home and for Valeria to go to bed.

It wasn't the attention she craved.

She wants over two minutes focused on her.

Valeria stares at the bowing, water-stained ceiling and wonders what to do with her extra time this morning. She plays with her mess of brunette hair and pulls herself out of bed.

She stops by the dresser and picks up Aria's precious hairbrush. She twists the handle, and a smile tickles her lips. *It'd be so easy to snap it into pieces.* She looks to Aria's bed. *To leave it in pieces in her sheets? Or to break it in front of her?*

Valeria runs the brush through her hair and tosses it back on the dresser. She has time to think about it and leaves the bedroom for the back of the house.

"Valeria?" her mother calls, holding a cup of coffee over the kitchen sink. "What are doing home?"

"I'm leaving soon," Valeria says, opening the back door. She smiles and adds, "I'm tried from my date last night."

Her mother gasps, slamming her cup on the kitchen bench. "What did you do with that boy? It was your first date."

Valeria tingles from her mother's reaction. Her eyes flick to the *Aria shrine.* Her parents don't flat out call it that, but they may as well. The shelves proudly host Aria's medals and trophies from childhood to now. Valeria's are shoved to the side. Her imagination grows dust, cobwebs and spiders over her achievements.

She moves space between the trophies in the centre of the middle shelf and smiles, envisioning a tall trophy with *Valeria Rivera* inscribed over *National Swimming Champion.*

She walks outside, closing the door behind her. Her mother's overactive thoughts would be better fun than whatever Valeria could respond with.

She walks across the lawn to the small tool shed that sits by the warped fence line. The tin door creaks open, and the dimly lit space feels like home. Her father cleaned pools for a living to make ends meet, but since he started training her and Aria for the State Championships, he gave up work. He puts everything into swimming training and ignores everything else.

Valeria seized the opportunity to occupy the space. The work bench displays her favourite possessions. A rusted wrench, a chipped hammer, miscellaneous lengths of rope, and bent and crudely sharpened nails.

Dating is a curse. I'm not stupid enough to fall for it. Pa is testing my loyalties. But now I must work harder for his attention. He doesn't want to know me because I didn't qualify for Nationals. But I'll make him see me. He won't be able to miss me.

Valeria struts towards the pool after her leisurely morning. She eyes her father, who watches Aria's freestyle technique.

Here we go.

Valeria is giddy. She's longed for this moment when her father snaps his head towards her and she's his entire focus. She doesn't care if he yells loud enough for everyone to hear. It will be visible proof he cares about her.

She can't hide her smile. Her excitement is too massive to push down.

Her father's eyes don't budge from the pool.

Valeria stands a few metres away, praying for him to turn. She clears her throat. Stamps her foot. Huffs. None of them work.

Her father fixates on her sister.

Just like he always does.

Valeria focuses on Aria, who glides through the water.

She has to pay.

"What are you doing?" her father grumbles.

Valeria's heartbeat speeds when she realises the grumble is aimed at her.

"I'm here now," she says, breathlessly.

His gaze stays on the water. "Get in the water then."

That's it? That's all I get?

She waits, biting her lip, hoping he'll yell or at least look at her.

Nothing.

"I was tired from my date," she says with hope.

"Mhmm," is all he replies.

Irritation buzzes in her veins. She balls her hands into fists and marches to a bench. She takes off her sweatsuit and pulls on a swimming cap.

Fine. I'll prove myself in the water.

Valeria punches the water when she finishes her last lap. She looks to the side of the pool where her father stands, shaking his head at the stopwatch in his hand.

He doesn't even look at her.

Every lap, it distracted her, trying to see if her father noticed her technique. She knows being bad in the water doesn't work. It only makes her invisible.

Her father's eyes go back to Aria, who is on her extra laps.

Dear God, please make her runaway. Aria needs to quit swimming and leave home forever. It's the only way my parents will pay any attention to me.

Amen.

Valeria pulls herself out of the water and paces to her towel. She watches the adoration in her father's eyes as he watches Aria's strokes. Her grip on the towel intensifies to the point it tears.

She bites her tongue and tastes the metallic, seeping blood.

She needs to increase her efforts in provoking Aria, or her dreams can't come true. She needs Aria to realise she's unwanted. If Valeria doesn't compete in the Championships, she will never be her parents' hero. There will be no point to her existence.

Valeria stands tall, knowing her only mission is to take her sister's place in the Championships.

Moonlight

Aria didn't think she'd fall asleep, but after hours of tossing and turning, her vision falls into a field of lilies. She runs her hands in and around the flowers and looks up at a rainbow coloured sky. When her gaze dips down, she's met with sparkling green eyes. She smiles until the eyes turn to fire. In confusion, she asks what's going on, until the fire grows intense. So intense her hair becomes the flames. The flames burn her scalp. Her scalp rips like it's being pulled.

She wakes, screaming in pain.

She opens her eyes to darkness, and her hair still feels like it's being severed from her scalp.

A hand slaps over her mouth and a face slides by hers. "Be quiet," her sister whispers. "Don't wake the rest of the house."

Valeria's hand pushes against Aria's nose and mouth, and panic courses through Aria's body. Valeria pulls her by the hair again. This time so forcibly, Aria falls out of bed.

Valeria picks her up and keeps her hand sealed over Aria's mouth. "Come with me," Valeria says. "We're ending this."

Twisting her auburn hair and pinching the skin at the back of her scalp, Valeria pushes Aria through the house and out to the backyard.

She throws her to the ground and orders her to stay there.

"What are we doing?" Aria pleads.

Aria's heart thumps against her ribs as she squints under the shadowy moonlight. Sweat trickles down Aria's nose and her fingernails dig into the barren ground.

Valeria marches towards the tool shed.

Her heart plummets to her stomach and the air sucks out of her lungs.

The tool shed door swings open, and Valeria paces towards her. A wrench twirls in one hand, a hammer swings in the other.

"Wh-Wh... What are you doing?" Aria stammers. Fear turns her blood cold.

"It's time you knew what it was like," Valeria says, stopping in front of her.

"Knew what?"

Valeria thwacks the wrench into Aria's shoulder.

Aria cries out in pain, but Valeria talks over her.

"To know what it's like to be cast a side. I'm the older sibling. I should be the one getting Pappa's praise." She whacks Aria again and this time the blow sends Aria backwards. "You should never have been born!"

Aria grips her shoulder, wincing in pain. "I'm sorry. Valeria, I'm sorry. I'll get out of swimming. I'll do whatever you want."

Valeria drops the wrench and twirls the hammer, a smile curling her lips. "Oh, you won't be swimming. I'm making sure of that."

"Please," Aria whimpers.

"You're the reason everything is wrong," Valeria says, stepping a foot on either side of Aria's legs. "You're the reason Ma's always crying. You're the reason we had to leave church. You're the reason we have no money." Valeria lifts the hammer high. "You're the reason for everything bad in my life. Everything is your fault!"

"Stop!" Aria pleads. Tears sting her eyes as she wriggles away from her sister. "Valeria, please! I'm sorry."

Valeria swings the hammer. "You stole everything from me!"

Aria's eyes bulge with shock as the hammer soars towards her knee. She reacts quick enough to pull her knee out of the firing line. Valeria almost loses balance as the hammer ploughs into the dirt.

Valeria pulls the hammer up and the moonlight shines against the glimmering hatred in her eyes.

She takes another swing, and Aria watches the hammer aim for her shin. Aria pulls her leg toward her torso, but the hammer connects with her body. The hammer splinters her ankle and excruciating pain radiates up her leg.

Valeria lets out a high pitch scream and thrashes the hammer against Aria's ankle two more times.

Aria screams out as her ankle burns and fractures under her skin.

"My lord, what has happened?"

Valeria tosses the hammer as she turns around to see her father at the back door.

"There was a man," Valeria rushes, standing up. "He took us from our beds. I tried to fight him off. But he got Aria."

"Aria!" Angelo cries, running towards them. He turns to his wife, who whimpers inside the house. "Call the police!"

Angelo runs to the girls and drops by Aria. "How did this happen?"

"It all happened so quickly," Valeria answers.

Aria lets out another scream of pain. The pain is bigger than her body.

Angelo strokes Aria's hair, and asks, "Did you see who it was?"

Aria's eyes fog with hot tears. She squints at her sister lurking by her father's side. She shakes her head, the pain extreme and overwhelming.

"No, I didn't see them." She grits her teeth to bear the pain. "Happened too quickly."

Pressure

Eddy's gut twists as he towels off after his swim. It's been days since he last saw the red-haired girl and her family at the pool. It's unlike them to skip a day. He'd overheard they were championship swimmers, and with a competition fast approaching, it's odd for them to not be in the water.

The brunette sister walks behind her father, and Eddy exhales. His stomach unclenches as he searches for that gorgeous auburn hair.

She's nowhere in sight.

Her sister locks eyes with him and smiles. Eddy smiles back, hoping she will give him a clue to where the missing girl is.

He glances at the father, and an unsettling feeling washes through his core. The father seems distant, and his eyes avoid the water.

The brunette sister saunters towards Eddy, a flirty glint to her eyes, and tosses her chocolaty hair over her shoulders.

"Hey there," she says with a bounce.

"Hi," Eddy replies.

"I've noticed you've been checking me out," she says with her hands clasped behind her back.

Eddy rubs the back of his neck. "Uh..."

She giggles and touches his arm. "Don't feel bad. I don't blame you for looking at me. But I really need to concentrate." She drops her hand and sits it on her hip. "My father said I can date, but he's going to take it back now. I'm in training to become the new National swimming champ, so I really need you to stop being a distraction."

Eddy tries to remove the dumbfounded expression from his face. "Ok."

"Seriously, boy, stop staring at me."

"I will. Sorry for distracting you."

She pops her knee, posing in front of him. "Good."

When she doesn't leave, and her sister isn't around, Eddy decides to probe a little deeper. "How's everything at home?"

The girl's lip upturns. "Huh?"

"You and your family have been absent for a few days."

She bites her lip and smiles deviously. "So, you have been keeping tabs on me?"

"Is your father good to you?"

The flirty exterior vanishes, and offence coats her face. "Yes, of course. Why would you ask that?"

"Is your sister away at the moment?" Eddy presses. "Or at home?"

The girl almost gags. "How dare you!" she says loud enough for onlookers to turn. "Don't you dare pry into my family. What's the matter with you? You freak!"

She storms off, ripping off her t-shirt, ready to dive into the water.

Eddy's gaze moves back to the father, whose drawn face absent-mindedly looks to the bench seating.

Something bad has happened.

Eddy needs to find out more on this family. Something's definitely not right. He stares at the father's face, trying to work out the emotion. *Guilt? Fear? Remorse?*

His gut cramps as his worries for the singing sister intensify.

The way the light hit the autumn tones of her hair, and the way her sun-kissed tan played against her freckles, consumes his thoughts all day. His stomach flips as his mind tussles with work and the missing girl.

A knock at his door pulls him from his thoughts and Jazz walks into his office.

"You don't mind me coming in, do you?" Jazz asks.

Eddy rubs the back of his neck and is quick to reply, "No, not at all."

"You seem a little rattled," she says, taking a seat on the couch. "How are you today?"

"Good. Busy, but good," he replies. "Did we have a session?"

She nods, smiling, and sweeps her jet-black hair off her bare, olive shoulders. "Wednesday, one-thirty. Our standing appointment."

Eddy pinches the bridge of his nose and nods. "Geez, you're right. I had it in my head it was Monday."

Jazz tilts her head. "Are you sure you're ok, Eddy? That's not like you."

He waves it off, and says, "I'm fine. More importantly, how are you? Have you contacted your father yet?"

Jazz smooths down her skirt, fidgeting in place. "Not yet. I don't feel I have enough to report yet."

"It's not about reporting," Eddy says, leaning his elbows on his desk. "Remember, you're greeting a family member, not holding a business meeting."

Jazz huffs, playing with her hair. "It's not that simple. All we've ever talked about is dollars and numbers. It'll be the first thing he asks about."

"But this isn't a business. It's not-for-profit."

Her frown intensifies. "I know, but he won't care. I need the stats to see how many people are coming in and out. Who we help and how they make something of themselves in the community. And, who comes back for more refuge." Her dark almond eyes meet his with determination and a hint of hesitation. "Eddy, this place needs to work."

"Jazz, it's not—"

"—I'd like you to interview another therapist," Jazz cuts him off.

"What?"

"We need more hands on deck," she says, getting up and pacing. "I'll plug the position on my Collage feed, and I need you to vet their credentials and experience."

"Jazz, I don't think—"

"—We need this place humming like a well-oiled machine," she says, slapping a fist into her palm. "I need more manpower."

Eddy sits back in his chair and sighs as he rubs his temples. "Sure."

"So, you'll conduct the interviews?"

"Have you talked to Adrian about this?"

"He asked me to take care of the financial and staffing areas so he could focus on the face-to-face with new arrivals," Jazz says, curiously sheepish. "I'm doing what he asked."

Eddy straightens and finds her eyes. "The three of us should sit down and discuss this."

Jazz frowns and nods. "You're right. I need to stop being emotional and start getting focused."

Eddy puffs a laugh. "Excuse me? You think you're being too emotional?"

Jazz *tsks* and her eyes roll. "My connection to Myra is too overpowering. It's affecting how I think. I want to put the emotion aside and focus in on finding her before it slows me down."

"And why do you think being emotional will slow you down?"

Jazz presses into her stomach and swallows slowly. "Because it's sad. I don't like it." Jazz shakes it off and sits down. "I want finding Myra to be a success story. I want my father to hear about the great work I'm doing here."

"And you think your father will only be proud of you after you find Myra?"

Jazz huffs and falls back against the couch.

"Take your time processing your feelings. Don't rush them. Last time we talked, we touched on your mother. Are you still letting her presence into your life?"

"I don't want to talk about my mother."

"What makes you say that?"

"I thought I was like her, but maybe I was wrong."

"Jazz, you made so much progress in breaking down your barriers. Don't build them back up."

Jazz runs her hands over her face. "I need to fix this place first. Then I can think about my mother."

"You found your connection to your mother in this place. Forgetting her isn't the answer."

Jazz smirks. "I thought there were no wrong answers?"

Eddy smiles. "Jazz."

"I know what you're saying. There's just been so much transition in my life. It's hard keeping up with everything."

"I know. You're doing tremendously well."

"Thank you."

"I have an exercise I think would be beneficial for you. Would you give it a try?"

"What is it?"

"Writing a letter to your mother."

Jazz's face screws up. "My mother? She's dead."

"I'm aware," Eddy says gently. "Write to her spirit. Write what you've always wanted to say to her. Or simply, ask her for guidance. It could help a lot."

"I don't know."

Eddy slides a pen and paper across the desk. "Try?"

Jazz nods and takes the pen and paper. "I'll try."

He smiles. "Good."

She cracks her neck and asks, "Will you be ok to conduct the interviews if I line them up?"

"Let's take it one step at a time."

Jazz lifts the pen and paper. "I'll take these into Adrian's room. See if I get inspired."

"That's great."

Jazz thanks him and leaves his office, cutting their session short.

He exhales with relief. He's grateful for her help, especially for how she's helped ground his best friend, Adrian. But she's working him to the bone.

Eddy tries to stay reasonable and reminds himself she's putting pressure on him to mask her own insecurities. But when that pressure bleeds out from their sessions and into his work schedule, it becomes increasingly harder to not take it personally.

Classic

Jazz places her shoes on a rack by the entrance and enters the mosque. She breathes in the cool crisp air and smiles at the comfort from the soft maroon carpet under her feet. She fixes the scarf covering her raven hair and pulls her sleeves down to her wrists. Her ankle-length skirt tugs around her legs as she walks towards the worshippers.

She kneels on the carpet and gazes at those around her. Her fingers flex on her lap, and a quiver of guilt sloshes in her gut, reminding her of the years passed since she last attended temple. She takes a cue from those around her and dips her head in silent reflection.

This is the third time Jazz has come to the mosque hoping to find Tazbir. He's the father of Myra, who she met a few weeks ago at the shelter. A girl who sparked a newfound purpose in her. A girl with a young son and running from an abusive partner.

Jazz's heart aches for Myra and her son's safety and desperately wants to help her. She hopes Myra has returned to her family. It's hard to know for sure when Jazz is unaware of Myra's family name.

After a few silent minutes, Jazz stands and moves to the front of the mosque. She collects her shoes and steps onto the top of the stone steps. A group of men in cream and tan robes stand in a group on the cement path below. She takes a quick inhale and makes her way over to the group.

She clasps her hands together, standing a metre away from them. One man notices her and clears his throat. The rest of the men turn and take her in.

"Can we help you, Miss?" one man asks.

Jazz straightens her back and smooths down the waist of her skirt. "Sorry to bother you, but I was wondering if any of you were, or know of, a Tazbir?"

"Tazbir?" one man with a grey and black-patched beard asks. "Why's that?"

Jazz swallows dryly and says, "It's about his daughter."

The man takes a step forward. "Myra?"

Jazz's eyes round and her chin drops. "Yes. She's your daughter?"

Tazbir holds a hand out to the side, gesturing for her to step away with him. "When did you see her last?"

"A few weeks ago."

"Is she ok?"

Sadness fills Jazz's veins. "I'm not sure. She was in a bad way when I saw her. So, she hasn't returned home?"

Tazbir's frown pulls down all the creases in his aged face. "Not in three years."

Jazz rubs her palm over her heart. "I'm sorry, this must be painful. I was really hoping you'd heard from her."

"Is that horrible punk hurting her?"

"I met her when she'd left him." She pauses, scared of her next words. "But I'm worried he found her again."

Jazz wills the tears not to show, wanting to be strong in front of Tazbir. The story Myra told her about her relationship with Danny haunts her thoughts. She hopes if Myra is hiding; she left Maiden City. She left and Danny is still here, waiting for his comeuppance.

Jazz pulls a card from the pocket of her skirt. "This is my phone number," Jazz says, giving the card to Tazbir. "Will you call if you hear from her?"

Tazbir nods. "I will. Please come back and tell me if you find her."

Jazz smiles and nods, taking in the concern and love in the man's eyes. Myra said she came from a good family. Close-knit and comforting. She rebelled and threw away the relationships with her family members for a bad boy. Looking in Tazbir's eyes, Jazz knows he will forgive all if Myra shows up on his doorstep. He misses his daughter, and Jazz wonders how her own father is feeling about her. If he misses her?

"You look perplexed," Tazbir says.

Jazz shakes out of her thoughts. "No, it's nothing."

"Were you and Myra close? You seem to take this personally."

Jazz chews her lip and huffs. "It'd be sad if Myra didn't return home. I feel you'd make a great father."

Tazbir takes her in, folding his arms. "When's the last time you saw your father?"

Jazz gazes at the mosque and replies, "A few weeks."

"Go see your father," Tazbir says gently. "You look like you're missing a piece of yourself."

Jazz thanks Tazbir and hopes to see him again soon. Her pace is sluggish along the cement path as the painful decision to leave her father's company settles on her shoulders. It is paramount the shelter becomes successful. Jazz's worst fear is returning to her father with her tail between her legs because her venture was a failure. A humiliation she cannot bear.

Meeting Myra and Taz awakened the maternal, feminine piece of herself she never knew existed. She needs to find them soon, before that piece dies. Her hand fishes in the pocket of her skirt and grabs a hold of the letter.

There's so much guilt and sadness with her mother. Her mother died giving birth to her, and she hates feeling like the reason she died.

Being around Adrian has strengthened this new side of her. Her empathetic side. Her patient side.

Patience is something she still needs to work on, but she is getting there. Adrian is still putting up with her, so she can't be doing that bad.

Dear Mother,

This is so crazy, but I'll give it a go. I really wish I could have met you. I'm not sure if you ever held me in your arms. I'm sorry for that. You were excitedly looking forward to becoming a mother. Nine months to prepare, and then my arrival takes it all away. I'm so sorry.

Father misses you. I can tell by the way he doesn't talk about you. A bad habit I picked up. It's hard for us. We don't like to show emotion. Eddy just looked at me like I'm stupid for wanting my emotions to go away. But they are getting in the way. I want to shut them down like Father taught me. Look at things like business stats so I don't fall apart inside.

I need to find Myra. Myra helped me get in touch with my true self. Her sweet baby boy. Ah, to see his face again. I might want a child of my own one day. That's what makes me think becoming a mother would have excited you. I think I got the feeling from you.

I know Father thinks I made a mistake leaving his company. I think he assumes I'm going to be a failure without him. I need to show him it's not a mistake and that I'm doing well on my own. I'm happy here. I'm making a difference. Shouldn't that be enough?

Your daughter,

Jazz

When she returns to the shelter, Jazz quickly changes into a knee-length pencil skirt and sheer, lemon blouse. The news crew will be at the shelter in a matter of minutes and she needs to put her best foot forward.

Father could see this. Game face on.

"Adrian," she calls out, jogging up the hall to catch him.

Adrian turns around, his trademark cheery smile brightening his face. "Hey, you're back."

Jazz lands by him, scoops his hand in hers and keeps her pace brisk, dragging him with her. "Channel Six will be here soon. We need to get ready."

"We?" Adrian questions. "I'm not going on camera."

Jazz smooths over his light brown hair, and says, "Not looking like this. You want to change into that outfit I bought you?"

As Adrian side-eyes her, she clicks her tongue, knowing he won't dress up at the shelter.

"Fine, you can go for that rugged, authentic look," she says, giving him a wink.

Adrian squeezes her hand. "How did it go at the mosque?"

Jazz's heartbeat speeds up, and she stops dead. "I found Tazbir."

Adrian stops with a jerk and his jaw drops. "You're kidding."

Jazz can't hide the sadness from her expression. "Myra hasn't returned to her family."

Adrian frowns and wraps his arms around her. "I'm sorry."

Jazz takes in his warmth, but when he goes to kiss her, she breaks free of him. "We don't have much time. I have to get ready."

Adrian fidgets as she creates distance between them. "Ok."

"Sorry, I'm just a little stressed."

"You don't have to do this right now," Adrian suggests. "The Myra thing has rattled you. The last thing you need is a camera in your face."

Jazz shakes her head and keeps moving towards the communal dining room. "No, the shelter needs this. We need the word out to increase our funding efforts."

Jazz hurries her pace into the dining room and pivots her gaze to check all the surfaces are as clean as she left them. No rubbish or clutter lying around. *Perfect.*

"Jazz," Gene says, walking into the dining room. "Jenna from Channel Six is here." Jazz turns to Gene in time for him to halt and drop his jaw at Adrian. "Why do you look like that? You told me you were gonna change."

Adrian laughs and turns away from Gene. "I'm not going on camera. Don't fuss about me."

Gene exaggerates his huff and moves toward Jazz. "It's TV, Adrian. Jazz, you look magnificent."

Jazz smiles. "Thank you."

"Jazz Abadi?" Jenna, from Channel Six, asks, strutting into the room with a cameraman behind her.

"Yes," Jazz says, extending her hand. "Nice to meet you."

Jenna shakes her hand. "You too. Shall we get started?"

"Of course."

Jenna gets underway with her interview questions. "So, what made you want to take on this project?"

"This shelter was already established," Jazz replies. "But it terribly needed funding. After spending some time here, I felt it my duty to repay the community."

"What lead to your initial time here?"

A laugh escapes Jazz as she answers, "A really turbulent time in my life. Bottom line, even though I was from an affluent part of Maiden City, the people here treated me as one of their own. Rich, poor, man, woman, everyone is welcome to seek solace, privacy, and protection under this roof."

"And, can you elaborate on the origins of the refuge centre?"

"Adrian," Jazz says, beckoning him over to the spotlight. "Come over here."

Adrian backs away, waving his hands. "No, you're doing fine."

Jazz deadpans at him, unintentionally stomping her foot. She covers, clearing her throat and grinning at Jenna.

With a glance from Gene, Adrian steps forward and makes his way to Jazz and Jenna.

"Adrian? You're the founder?" Jenna asks.

Adrian eyes Jazz, and then the camera, lost for words.

Jazz pats Adrian's arm and plasters her Collage smile. "Yes, Adrian Cassidy started up the centre. If it weren't for people like him, this city would surely collapse."

"Wow, you sound like quite a guy," Jenna says, tilting the microphone toward Adrian. "It must be a thrill to have Jazz Abadi's endorsement. Is it true you two are a romantic item?"

Light flickers in Adrian's brown eyes and his smile returns.

Jazz stops him as his first word touches his lips. "This is more a case of our business relationship than anything else."

Jenna laughs. "Classic Jazz Abadi, all business."

After the interview, and Jenna and her cameraman leave, Jazz takes a long breath out. "Wow, that went well." She looks for Adrian and his arms lock against his chest. "What?"

"Why couldn't I say we were dating?" he asks.

Jazz smooths over her hair, looking away. "My father could be watching."

"And?"

"And, I don't want a local news piece twisted with a romance. I've told you how business focused he is." Jazz glances at Adrian's attire. *Imagine father's words if he saw him like this.* "You understand, don't you?"

Adrian's jaw clenches, but he soon releases and nods. "Shouldn't it be about us, not him?"

"Mhmm." Jazz nods. "Of course."

Expected

"**Adrian**?" Jazz questions, a surprised smile to her lips as she enters his office. She's clutching the card he had Gene leave for her.

Adrian smiles, heat colouring his face as he lights the last of three candles on his desk. "Good, you got my invite."

"What is all this?" she asks as the candlelight plays against her olive complexion.

"Some time for just the two of us," Adrian says, rounding the desk and clasping her hand. "You know, trying to *woo* you."

Jazz giggles and squeezes his hand. "I like that."

Adrian leads her to a chair and pulls it out for her. When Jazz sits, Adrian retrieves two plates from atop the filing cabinet and places them on his desk. "A little birdy told me you like Italian food."

Jazz's eyes dazzle as she takes in a whiff of fettuccine Alfredo. "This smells just like St Paolo's."

Adrian's chest puffs with confidence. "It is."

Shock fills Jazz's face. "What?"

"I got Gene to do some digging. He already knows so much about you," Adrian says as Jazz's eyes stay entranced on his. "I wanted to get you food from your favourite place."

"But it's expensive," Jazz whispers, guilt slouching her. "You shouldn't have. I'm sure Hector could have cooked—"

Adrian lifts a hand to stop her sentence. "Nah-uh. Hector cooks every night. This one has to be special."

"Why tonight?"

"Why not every night?"

Jazz giggles and reaches her hand across the desk to snag his. She laces their fingers together and looks deeply into his eyes. "Thank you, it's wonderful."

They twirl at their pasta and after a few bites, Adrian laughs and jokes, "This won't mix well with the jogging kick you've got me on."

Jazz nods. "Pasta are carbs, and carbs help you burn off energy. As long as you don't keep surprising me with rich foods, we should be able to keep healthy."

"So, you don't want the double-fudge chocolate cake for dessert?" Adrian teases.

Jazz sucks in her lips and moans. "Yum." She exhales and says, "I want that so badly."

"But, really," Adrian says, steadying his voice to match his sincerity. "Thank you so much. You've made me feel so much more stable since you've been here. I'm not so crazy in my head and feel a lot calmer."

Jazz nods, maintaining eye contact. "Physical exercise works wonders for mental health."

"You know it's more than that," Adrian adds. "Yeah, I'm glad you've gotten me into a routine, but it's you that's made everything better."

"I could say the same," Jazz says, glancing down at the food and then back at him. "Thank you for letting me into your world. I'm one-hundred percent a better person for it." She blows out a breath and looks to the side. "It's just the Myra and Taz stuff that keeps getting me unstuck."

Adrian tenses, hoping to have an evening where Myra and her son don't take up their entire conversation.

"How's the food?" he haphazardly tries for a change of subject.

"It's great," she says, twirling her fork. "Just as I remember it."

Adrian's stomach pangs, and he asks, "You don't miss that lifestyle? Going out to fancy dinners and having business meetings?"

Jazz smiles and reaches across to touch his face. "I have fancy dinners and business meetings. Buffet-style in the dining room that I get the pleasure of washing up after, and meetings with Eddy about hiring more staff."

"More staff?"

Jazz bats a hand. "Oh, it's nothing. I have some more ideas to expand the shelter and I'll bring them to you when they are finalised."

"Oh, ok."

"Don't think I'm here and missing out on things. I'm here because I want to be here."

Adrian's chest fills with air and his heart bounces. "That's good." His hands tremble and he tries to shake off the nerves as Jazz goes back to her food. "I love you, Jazz."

Jazz twirls at her pasta, flicking her hair over her shoulder.

Did she hear me?

His knee bounces nervously. He waits for her to look up, but she takes a bite of dinner instead. Her eyes are off to the side like her mind's adrift.

"Are we ok?" he asks when she finishes eating her mouthful.

She smiles cheerily. "Of course. Why?"

"Oh, nothing."

They finish their meals, and questions plague Adrian.

She doesn't love me.

Why would she love me?

She wants someone successful and well-educated, like Ethan Roth.

"Dessert?" Jazz asks, light dancing in her eyes like an excited child.

"Sure," he says, changing their plates out for dessert.

"I can't stop thinking about Myra," Jazz says, defeated. "Why wouldn't she return home to her family? They were so loving and supportive. Anyone would give for a situation like that."

"Nothing is ever what it seems on the surface."

"What?"

"It might seem idyllic to you, but people would have said the same about your life."

Jazz slumps in her chair. "I guess you're right."

"There's a reason she's running, and maybe you have to let her run?" Adrian suggests, but he immediately regrets it when he sees the look in her eyes.

Adrian gulps and worries he's miss-stepped. *Again.* Jazz is independent and determined. He knows that stopping her vision or ideas for the shelter could make her flee. He likes giving her the reins to make her happy.

Happy enough to stay with him.

"Sorry," he says. "You do what you think is best."

Jazz straightens up. "Thank you."

After their dinner, Adrian walks Jazz out so he can watch her safely get into her driver's car.

Chaos buzzes through the hall. He settles a hand on the small of Jazz's back and as they pass the T in the hall. He looks down the dining room and grows queasy. He's noticed some people in the shelter who don't seem to need their help. There were groups of people who looked as if they could be from Jazz's neighbourhood.

The new influx of people is massive. Adrian didn't know if he's capable of talking to each person one-on-one.

He looks to the other end of the hall, and spots Gene rushing out of the common room. "Genie?" he asks, moving his hand from Jazz. "Are you ok?"

"Don't go up there," Gene says, waving his hands frantically. "It's crazy-town in there."

Adrian tilts his head to take in the commotion. "What's happening?"

"There's a bunch of preppy douchebags starting up a beer-pong tournament on the pool table."

Adrian's eyebrows lift as his eyes grow circular. "What? That's not ok."

Gene grabs Adrian's shoulders and looks square in his eyes. "Aid, breathe for me. Take a chill pill and breathe. Don't go in there panicked, you won't control the room."

Adrian looks in Gene's dark eyes, and a wave of calm washes over him. It doesn't last long when the voices fill his surroundings again, but he feels slightly lighter.

"Thanks, Genie," Adrian says, patting Gene's back. "What the hell are preppy guys doing here? This is a shelter for vulnerable people."

Gene shrugs. "Something in Jazz's message must have sparked something. Maybe they didn't hear she was running from harm. Maybe they saw a rich person hanging out somewhere and became invisible."

Adrian grits his teeth and his stomach clenches. He did not like where this was going.

Are they looking for somewhere to lay low from their parents? Do they think they can get drugs here?

Adrian's head fills with more questions and he backs away to give himself a moment to think. He should venture to the common room and check who's in there, but noise at every end of the shelter pulls at him.

"Adrian?" Jazz says and touches his arm.

Adrian flings her off and steps away.

"*Whoah*," Jazz says. "Are you ok?"

"I knew that interview was a bad idea," he snaps.

Her eyes round. "What?"

Adrian gestures round him. "People should be able to come here to hide and feel comfort," Adrian says, and edge to his words. "You took all that away with your cameras. You need to think of people's privacy."

"I did it so we could help more people," she argues.

"How is this help?" he asks, raising his voice.

"Hey," Gene hushes. "Chill out."

"I thought you would enjoy speaking to more people," Jazz says, her lip quavering.

Adrian takes in the soft angles of her face and his chest falls. As her shiny eyes stay locked on his, he instantly wants to take it all back.

"I'm sorry," he whispers, taking a step towards her.

She exhales and nods. "Ok."

They stare at each other in silence before she adds, "I'm going to go."

"I'll walk you out," Adrian says, moving to sling an arm around her shoulders.

Jazz slides away from him. "I got it."

"Jazz," he says in a hush. His heart sinks. "I'm sorry. I didn't mean what I said."

Jazz nods. "I know."

Without a smile or a frown, Jazz turns and makes her way out the front door.

"What happened?" Gene asks, shock changing his face. "Didn't tonight go well? I thought she'd love it."

Adrian shakes his head and looks away from the door. "I dunno."

Gene grabs Adrian's arm. "What is it?"

"Nothing," Adrian says, sliding his hand off. "Get to sleep, will you. You need to be fresh for your classes tomorrow."

"Ok," Gene says timidly.

Gene moves away towards his bedroom. Adrian slumps against the wall, trying to get himself sorted before he goes to the common room to break up the frat boy party.

His mind goes straight to the locket he took from her all those years ago.

She doesn't forgive me.

Jazz told him she forgave him, but the distance coming between them leads him to believe it's not true.

Does she want to break up with me?

The words pull at his battered heart.

Should I end things first?

It kills him that Jazz keeps him out of the loop. He doesn't understand why they don't work on things together. They talk about the shelter, but never their relationship.

He expected to hear the words *I love you* from her lips tonight. He wants to make her happy. He'll apologise and let her keep moving forward the way she wants.

Maybe that will bring us closer.

Halo

Aria drags the moon boot encasing her screwed-together ankle across the concrete as her heart sits heavily against her chest. Her breaths are laboured, exhausted from everyone talking about her lack of swimming and less about her recent attack.

She was in hospital for two days after her surgery. They realigned her ankle using metal rods, screws, and a plate. The moon boot helps her walk, but it feels like she's dragging a hunk of metal with her, not a piece of her body.

No swimming. It rips away the only thing that brought a shred of meaning to her life. The glee in Valeria's eyes has been unmistakable. She was told by officials she now placed in the National Championships.

Now I truly am useless, Aria thought, *just as Valeria always said. I am nothing without the water.*

Aria doesn't have any friendships, so in this time she is truly alone. Except for Valeria's cruel words taking up residence in her mind.

She told the police what she had told her father. That a man took her and her sister from their beds. That he had a mask on. That it was dark. That it was quick.

She protected her sister because family comes first.

When her father brought her home from the hospital, Aria hobbled to her bedroom for rest. She went to the dresser to pick up her beloved hairbrush, but it was missing.

It didn't surprise her Valeria touched or moved it.

She sat on her bed and something jagged poked into her thigh. Her mind scattered to pieces of metal hidden in the bedding. She moved and pulled back the bedcover. Broken in pieces was her hairbrush. The one thing in the room truly hers and brought her joy. Lay in shards.

Today she took the bus to the swimming pool. The house felt tiny, and she needed to get out. Her bedroom was confining when left alone with her tormenting thoughts.

Aria drags herself to the edge of the swimming pool. What is her self-worth without swimming? What is the point of living?

There is none.

Fully dressed, she closes her eyes and flings her body into the deep end. The moon boot drags her down. The water bubbles around her. She relaxes her limbs, giving no reaction to move to the surface.

Her body sinks to the bottom of the pool. She intakes a rush of water. Her auburn hair stretches away from her head. As she watches a lock wave by her eyes, arms scoop around her body.

Her body shoots out of the water. She squints at the sunlight and someone's arms pull her to the edge.

Onlookers help her out of the water. She hears someone getting out of the water beside her. She's placed on the cement. She coughs and splutters water out of her mouth. She gasps and coughs, loud and rough. A hand presses on the side of her neck.

"You're ok, you're ok," a caring, and slightly panicked, male voice says.

She spits out more chlorinated water and squints hard, trying to block out the sunlight and find the face the voice belongs to.

He leans over her, and the sun creates a halo effect around his dark blonde hair.

It's him.

"Can you sit up?" he asks.

"Help me," she says in a hoarse voice. "Can't go home."

He nods, looking into her eyes. "Ok, I'll get you out of here."

Trouble

Aria stirs awake. A smile tickles her lips as she stretches out on the plush mattress, sandwiched between silky smooth sheets. Her dream-state dissipates and her eyes shoot open.

She gasps, sitting up. She pulls the sheet to her chest, taking in the dusty pink walls and affluent decor. She looks down at the king-sized bed and trembles.

Where am I?

Under the sheet, she's wearing an oversized Maiden City University t-shirt. She tries to remember what happened before she went to sleep.

When did I go to sleep?

Where did I go to sleep?

Is Valeria here?

There's a knock on the bedroom door and it opens. "Hello?"

Aria screams on instinct, pulling the sheet up to her chin.

He enters quickly, hands out like stop signs. "Hey, hey, it's ok. You had an accident."

Aria drops the sheet, tilting her head. *I know him.* The same boy she kept seeing at the swimming pool. The short blonde hair, magnetic green eyes, slender face with high cheekbones, and that tall, slim body made for the water.

She opens her mouth to ask where she is, but her throat inflames, and her chest constricts. She flops back on the fluffy pillows behind her.

He sits at the end of the bed. "Do you remember being at the pool?"

Aria dips her head, pressing her fingertips into her forehead as she thinks back.

"You fell in," he elaborates.

Aria drops her hands and wonders how she got here, when he says, "I brought you here. You told me you couldn't go home, and no hospital."

Aria's heart drops and her stomach wobbles. *I said that?*

"Normally, when people tell me that, it means they are running from something," he says in a hushed tone. "Did someone hurt you?"

Aria's shock keeps her mute.

His eyes widen, and he gets off the bed.

He opens a different door, and it surprises Aria when it's a bathroom. *A bathroom in his bedroom? He must be rich.*

"I dried this for you," he says, retrieving her moon boot.

Aria reacts quickly, knowing she should wrap it around her foot. She pushes the sheet down, but pulls it back up at seeing the scandal of her bare legs.

"You don't remember coming here at all?" he asks hesitantly.

Aria gulps and shakes her head.

"I gave you the change of clothes," he says, keeping his distance. "I didn't weirdly dress you or anything."

Aria blows out a breath and lets herself smile.

She pulls the long t-shirt down to the tops of her thighs and slides down the ivory bed sheet. She winces at the sight of her mangled ankle.

"I wondered why I hadn't seen you at the pool lately," he says, slipping her foot back into the boot and buckling it up. "Looks like a nasty break."

Aria winces through the pain of her foot being moved. She exhales once it's secured.

He steps away from the bed, allowing Aria to pull the sheet back up. "Did it happen at home?"

The thought of answering him sends a panic throughout her body.

"Are you hungry?" he asks, lightening the mood with the subject change.

Aria touches her stomach and notes a gurgle. She laughs and nods.

His grin brightens the room. "Your laugh is as sweet as your singing voice."

An embarrassing heat rises on her face.

He hangs a thumb over his shoulder to the bathroom. "I have an extra set of clothes for you. They're some of mine, but you're a tall girl, so they should fit. Would you like to shower while I make breakfast?" He pauses for her to answer, and when she continues in silence, he says, "Or there's a tub in there if it's easier. You can decide what you want to do. Will you need help?"

The thought of him seeing her without clothes fills her with trepidation. She shakes her head violently, scrunching the bed sheets with her fingers.

"Call me if you need anything." He walks to the door. "My name is Eddy."

He leaves the room and Aria's heart swells from the sound of his name.

My gosh.

Aria flops back on the perfectly soft pillows and looks up at the hanging glass lighting.

He saved me?

She pulls herself out of bed and shuffles her way to the dusty pink, velvet armchair that's morphed into a clothes rack for a pair of track pants and a sweatshirt. Aria lifts the pants and holds them against her. She moves into the bathroom and her eyes enlarge as she takes in the sparkling tiles, double sinks, stone bathtub, and wide frosted glass shower.

She perches on the edge of the tub and runs a hand over the products in a basket. *Could I really have a bubble bath here?* She looks back into the bedroom. *Is this a palace? This bathroom is twice the size of my bedroom. How big is the rest of the house?*

Aria rubs a lock of hair between her fingers. The chlorine has soaked in and she hates unclean hair. She turns on the water to the tub and set the plug in place. She'd have a quick wash to clean her hair and remove the pool smell from her skin, then she'd dash out of here.

It's like plunging into the deep end, sinking into the tub. Aria flinches in the water, hanging her moon boot covered foot over the edge. Her mind rewinds to the pool. Throwing herself into the water. Making no action to reach the surface. She wanted it over. Her life. She wanted her life to be over.

Her shudder ripples through the water. It scares her she had gone through with it. It scares her she had so little control over her life. That when the one thing that made her life matter was gone, she didn't feel like living.

She takes in her surroundings again. She blows a hole in some soap bubbles and smiles.

I got out of home.

She sinks lower into the water.

I'm going to be in so much trouble.

Aria takes her time carefully putting on the clothes and then leaves the bedroom.

Sizzling, crispy bacon and pancakes tease her nostrils. She giggles and pats her gurgling stomach. She follows the smell and finds an impressive kitchen and Eddy with his back turned by the stove.

He looks over his shoulder and smiles. "Pancakes ok?"

Aria gathers her hair and combs it nervously over her left shoulder. "Yes, thank you." She finds her voice and notices the green of Eddy's eyes intensify. "My name is Aria, by the way."

Eddy smiles and nods. "It's nice to meet you."

"Are you sure it's ok I'm here?"

"It's fine with me as long as you're comfortable," he says, piling food on a plate.

"It's a nice change of scenery," Aria says, studying the stainless steel appliances, marble benches, and glass cabinets displaying expensive-looking items. "I didn't expect to end up in such a nice place. This is your house?"

Eddy shrugs. "I live here, but this apartment is owned by my parents."

"They don't live with you?"

"No, they own a lot of property."

Aria tries to minimise her shocked expression, but it's a hard task.

Eddy laughs. "They're the ones with the money, not me. You're not from this side of town?"

She stands by the bench and places her palms on the white and black-flecked surface to steady her nerves. "I'm from Hamlet."

Eddy slides a plate by her. "Take a seat on a stool."

She pulls out a stool from under the bench, and says, "I think it's been years since I've eaten pancakes."

"Oh boy, that's too long without pancakes."

"Yeah, I s'pose it is," she says, cutting a piece of bacon. "I'm always in training, so there are pretty strict rules about what I can and can't eat." She takes a bite and happiness ignites every cell in her body. "Oh, yum."

Eddy laughs, placing his plate opposite her. "Good. Always what a chef wants to hear."

"You're a chef?" Aria asks. She nods to a seat beside her. "You're not sitting?"

"I'm ok standing," Eddy says, keeping his distance. "No, I'm not a chef, just an expression. I'm a counsellor."

"Counsellor? Is that like a therapist?"

He nods with a mouthful of pancake. He smiles and gives himself a thumbs up.

Aria laughs at him and takes another bite.

"Sorry that being here made you so frightened when you woke up," Eddy says, looking down at his plate. "I told myself it was a bad choice to come back here, but work is chaotic at the moment."

"Your work?"

"I work at a refuge centre. I'd have taken you there, but it so overrun. I thought it might be too much for you after what you had just gone through."

Aria gulps and raises her shoulders to her ears. "Yeah, that."

"You can talk to me about it... if you want."

She shakes her head and takes another mouthful of food.

"So, training?" he changes the subject. "That's for swimming?"

She nods and glances at her swinging moon boot. "Not that I can do it anymore."

"You'll heal."

Aria's frown cements on her face. "Not in time. I'm out of the Championships."

Eddy finds her eyes. "I'm sorry. You were looking forward to it?"

"It was all I had."

"Do you go to school?"

She shakes her head. "I left high school early to train full time."

"That's the dream? To be a professional swimmer?"

"I guess. I won State. Nationals was the next step."

"I'm sorry. That must be tough not being able to compete after all that hard work."

Aria shrugs. "My family is taking it worse."

"Is that your dad that trains you?"

"Yeah. I feel bad I can't fulfil all his hard work for him."

"You mean your hard work?" Eddy says, placing his fork on the benchtop.

"He has accomplishments of getting me into competitions and winning them."

"But he sees it as you winning, right?"

"He's the one who got me there."

"How is he at home?"

Aria arches her eyebrow. "Do you know Pa?"

Eddy picks up his fork and shuffles his footing. "No, just wondering."

"I am glad to be away from home," Aria admits, cutting into a pancake. "I needed some space."

"If you need someone to talk to, I'm here to listen."

"My swimming is very important to my family," Aria says cautiously. "It's a tough subject, me being out of the water."

"Your sister is still swimming?"

Stabbing pains attack Aria's heart at the mention of her sister. "She gets to take my place at Nationals." Aria sighs. "I hope my father can accept that."

"He's not happy for your sister?"

"It's a hard adjustment. He accepted she was out."

"But he can be happy she's back in and give you a rest."

"I guess."

"Are you resentful your sister is taking your place?"

Aria sits up and looks him dead in the eye. "Not at all. I wanted her to get in instead of me. I didn't want her to fail."

"Does your family see her as a failure?"

Aria swallows uncomfortably. "Well, she's not a winner."

"So, you're not upset about your sister?"

"Of course not. I love her. I prayed for her to place."

Eddy nods, his jaw flexing. He smiles and says, "Well, at least there's a silver lining for the family then."

Ritzy

Eddy told Aria to relax in the living room while he cleaned up. She offered to help, but her foot was aggravating her, so she happily crashed on a couch.

He still can't believe this beautiful girl is in his house.

She hadn't been at the pool in days, so he was imagining her standing on the edge of pool until he double checked.

A smile had tingled at his lips until he zoned in on her shattered expression. A sickly feeling rose from his stomach. He had noted the brace strapped to her foot, and before he could question why she was standing at the edge, she had flung her body forward.

In the moment, Eddy was all action. He needed to get to her and ensure she was safe. He had never felt more relief than when she coughed up water and took in air.

Once he finishes in the kitchen, Eddy joins Aria in the living room. He sits on the opposite end of the couch and watches her eyes gaze around the room.

"This place is so ritzy," Aria says.

Eddy rubs the back of his neck, embarrassed. "Yeah, it's ok."

"If you saw my house, you'd see this place as a palace."

"What's your house like?"

"Small," she says bluntly. She pauses and smiles. "I mean, it's home, so I like it, but maybe this apartment is bigger?"

"No way, this is a one-bedroom apartment."

"Yeah, and?"

Eddy laughs and relaxes on the couch. "As long as a place is homey, I guess. Nothing here is mine, it's just a place to sleep."

"You don't see it as home?"

Eddy shakes his head, taking in his surroundings. "It was my mother's place when she left my father for six months. She just left everything in here once she went back home."

"That's so sad your parents broke up," Aria says, her lips pouting.

"They go back and forth. It doesn't really phase me at this point." Eddy watches sadness droop her face. "Your family are tight-knit, I take it?"

Aria smiles. "Very." She looks off to the side, and asks, "Don't tell me home is one of those fancy mansions in Sovereign Hill?"

Eddy smirks. "No, they haven't staked a piece of land there, yet. I'm sure they'll keep working until they get there."

"You seem like you don't like it here."

"This is my parents' place, and this is their world. I stay here to keep the peace with them, but I don't share their values."

Aria runs her hand through her shiny red hair, and Eddy's mouth runs dry.

"I should probably get to work," Eddy says, pushing himself off the couch.

"Oh?"

"I'll only be gone a few hours," he says. "You can use that time to get some more rest. You've had quite a day. Unless you'd rather I take you home?"

"No," she's quick to respond. She smiles. "I'd like to stay. If that's ok."

He smiles back. "Yes, of course. Make yourself at home."

"Where is your work?"

"It's near The Limits. No one used to know about it, but then local TV news featured it and it became popular overnight. You should take advantage of the quiet and get some sleep."

"I'll try."

Eddy moves to a side table and picks up a short, laminated sheet. He hands to Aria and says, "If you need anything, here's a bunch of numbers you can call. I never really have food here, but call the top number and ask for anything you like. It's my parents' account and they're always wanting me to use it. If you're hungry, go ahead."

Aria looks at the sheet, bemused. "Ok."

Eddy taps a remote and adds, "And there are loads of movies and TV channels. I don't really know how it works because I'm never home to watch anything, but if you wanna figure it out, you're more than welcome."

Aria nods, her face awash with overwhelm.

Eddy gives her a reassuring smile. "Just try to get some sleep. I'll be back as soon as I can."

"Ok. Thank you, Eddy."

"You're welcome."

Chance

Valeria soaks in the freedom. Free from her little sister's shadow. It was a hard few days. Whilst Aria was in hospital, their parents' worship of her was unbearable.

Valeria never thought she'd find it a godsend to have her sister home, but at least it moved her father back to the pool and coaching her once again.

Her grin hurts as she powers through her laps, imagining her father's eyes on her and no one else. She slaps her hand against the tiles and looks up for her father's face.

He's not there.

Her expression drops, and she searches the pool's edge. Her father stands by the middle of the pool, eyes off at the deep end.

"Pappa!" she yells.

Her father shakes his head, awakening from his trance. He looks at her dumbfounded.

"Time!" she yells. "I thought I broke my PB."

She watches her father absent-mindedly hit the button of his stopwatch.

Valeria groans and punches the water.

What is the point of all that hard work?

Her rage bubbles inside her.

It's all Aria's fault. She still has his thoughts. She needs to disappear for good.

Valeria pulls herself out of the water, expecting an apology from her father.

"Aria can't spend this amount of time out of the water," Angelo murmurs, staring at water. "Twelve weeks, they told me. No swimming for twelve weeks."

Valeria grinds her teeth, suppressing her scream. She clears her throat and asks, "How did I do, Pa?"

"What will it mean for the Championships?" he continues like he didn't hear her. "She needs time to train."

"She won't be in the Championship!" she snaps. "She's out, I'm in. You train me to win the Championship."

Angelo's drawn, aged face turns to her for the first time. His exhausted, hollow eyes meet hers but don't seem to connect.

He moves to speak, but sighs instead, batting a hand at Valeria. He turns and walks away from her.

Valeria can't take it anymore. She stomps her foot on the hard, wet cement and lets out a scream. It rasps her throat and pierces her ears. It makes her feel better. She locks onto the pain and channels it into energy for when she gets home.

"Angelo," Keats, a fellow trainer, says as he walks up to them. "Sorry to hear about what happened to Aria."

Angelo's posture shatters. "Some sicko broke her ankle. I can't believe she's out of Nationals."

Keats shakes his head. "I'm talking about what happened this morning."

"This morning?" Angelo questions.

Valeria's ears prick, and she moves in closer.

"When she fell into the pool. How's she doing?"

"Fell in?" Angelo says. "Impossible. Aria is at home."

Keats shrugs. "It was definitely her. Took in some water, she did. She's having a rough go of it lately. The poor thing."

"Aria was here?" Angelo whispers, confusion spread across his face.

Valeria hugs her waist, a smirk tingling her lips. *Well, this is interesting.*

At home, the smile won't leave Valeria's face. She did it. She made Aria disappear.

Finally. Finally, it'll be all about me.

She walks into the kitchen and takes in the despondent faces of her parents, who sit at the dining table.

"What's wrong?" she asks, standing by the table.

"What's wrong?" her father snaps. "What are you, stupid?"

"Aria's missing," her mother shrieks in panic.

"The police won't do anything until she's gone forty-eight hours," her father says, staring at his laced hands. "Even though we already filed the report about the masked man attacking her."

Valeria scoffs. "And me, don't forget."

"This is so unlike her," Angelo continues, deep in thought. "She knows not to leave the home without permission. She should have told me where she was going. Why did she leave?"

"Can you stop focusing on her?" Valeria raises her voice, stomping her foot. "You know I'm standing here, right?"

"And what are you going to do?" Angelo yells, fury in his eyes.

Her mother bats a hand at her, rolling her eyes.

Valeria slaps her chest. "I'm about to compete in the National Championships! How about you turn your attention on me? We need to get me ready."

"You'd be ready if you swam better at the State competition," her father grizzles.

Valeria huffs and storms out of the room. *That's it, Aria. I need you gone for good.*

"Do you think she could be back at pool?" her mother asks her father.

Valeria circles back as her father tiredly says, "What would she be doing in the water with a moon boot on? It would make her sink. It makes no sense."

"We called the hospital," her mother adds. "She's not there. It must be a hoax."

Valeria chews her lip as her mind ticks. *Where are you, dear sister? We need to end this. Now.*

"Oh, where could she be," her mother wails, slamming her hands over her eyes.

"Oh, shut up," Valeria snaps.

Angelo stands, his chair hitting the ground. "Valeria!"

"Deal with her disappearance," Valeria yells, pacing toward them. She looms over her mother. "You deal with it before I make you."

"Did you do something to her?" Angelo asks, panicked as his wife cowers beneath their daughter.

"She left on her own, just as she should," Valeria says, whipping around to her father. "It's time you act like my father. You put the effort into working with me or I'll make sure she doesn't come back. Don't you want a chance to say goodbye?"

"Goodbye?" Angelo murmurs, collapsing to another seat. "We won't be letting her out of our sight."

"Make sure I win the Championship," Valeria lowers her tone, seething. "Forget Aria. I'll take care of finding her."

"Why are you doing this?" her mother whimpers, tears streaming from her eyes.

Valeria stands over her. "Want to test me? Or want to stay here where it's safe?"

Valeria watches them exchange terrified looks, and her grin

stretches. It hurts her face in a way that excites her.

Guilt

Aria finds it awkward being alone in Eddy's apartment. Her curiosity is more powerful than her need for sleep as she looks around the immaculate living area. The cream walls are lit with warmth from the perfect angles of the windows, gaining maximum sunlight.

Somehow the air feels fresher in this apartment. Her eyes wander across a metallic shelf housing minimalist black and white paintings and a tropical scent diffuser. She walks past the shelf and runs her hand along the broad leaves of a houseplant in a bronze and dust pink pot.

The apartment seems designed for a magazine shoot. Like no one should live here and all the items are will be shipped back to a furniture store display.

Her moon boot squeaks against the highly polished timber floors, and a rug sliding out from under the plush sofa is so stark white and incredibly soft, it could have been the coat of a polar bear.

She moves up the hall and her eyes draw up a feature of green and cream wallpaper that reminds her of the plants she passed earlier. Pressed against the wallpaper feature stands a cart of alcohol. She frowns and taps her fingernails against the glass bottles. Some stand half-empty and others are sealed shut. Aria tilts her head and takes in the array of drinks. With the little she knows about his mother, she wants to believe this bar also belongs to her.

She stops by an end table, showcasing photo frames. She leans over to examine the pictured events. She smiles on a picture of Eddy between two people who she suspects are his parents. They stand on a deck overlooking the beach with a perfect, orange-streaked sunset behind them.

Aria's smile drops, and she chews her lip. Her stomach spasms with guilt because she's left her family.

They don't know where I am.

They must be worried sick.

What am I doing?

This isn't me.

She turns around to find a phone. She moves into the next room and finds a desk with a laptop and phone. On her way towards it, she notices a plaque on the wall. *Edward Barnes*, it says proudly in the middle. Across the top states, *University of Maiden City.*

Aria stops and stares at the university degree. Her stomach stops flipping, and she stands taller. Her jaw clenches as anger heats inside of her.

My parents will never let me go to school.

She moves away from the phone and towards the kitchen. She pours herself a glass of water. Her hands trembles as she lifts the glass to her lips.

She puts the glass on the counter and watches the light reflect against the intricate design in blues and purples.

Fancy, she thinks, and pans around the room. The marble bench tops, the teardrop pendant lighting hanging from the ceiling, the chef-grade appliances.

Her stomach drops.

Everything is so fancy. It's too much, and I'm nothing.

She swallows hard and eyes grow glassy. *I don't belong here.*

This is so silly. I am stupid. Why would I dream about someone like him ever loving me?

He pities me.

I am another person for him to fix.

Comfy

Eddy keeps his head down when moving around the shelter. He wants to complete his work and then leave without taking on any new tasks.

"Hey Max," he says, walking back into his office to find Max sitting on his couch.

"Is it ok I just came in?" Max asks, slouching as he sits.

"Sure," Eddy says, sliding onto his desk to sit. "How are you doing today?"

Max bites his lip and fidgets in place.

"Max?"

"I went out today," Max starts, his body language unmistakably jittery. "Jazz and Adrian were talking at dinner one night about the best direction to go on a run, so I thought I'd give it a go."

"That sounds good," Eddy replies, trying to stay upbeat. "Exercise is a great way to maintain stress."

Max shrugs. "That's what they said, and yeah, it was pretty good."

"What's got you so agitated?"

He sighs and slides down the couch. "This guy from the Neons stopped me."

Eddy's jaw clenches and his back knots. "Did he threaten you?"

Max shakes his head, looking down. "Nah. Just had a message for me."

"From your brother?"

"He wants me to go back."

Eddy rocks his jaw, mulling his best response. "That's not what you want though?"

"I got out," Max says, determination pulling through his words. "But if Dean finds me... He could force me back."

Eddy slides off the desk and stands in front of Max. "I won't let that happen."

Max looks up at him, sadness watering his eyes. "I don't want to go back."

Eddy bends down and squeeze's Max's shoulders. "You stay inside these walls. We'll protect you. Like always."

Max frowns and looks to the door. "It's not like it used to be in here."

"I know," Eddy whispers. "We'll fix that. And, remember, a few weeks back we were going to shut this place down. We can make it work again."

Max nods. "I believe you. Hey, I wanted to talk to Adrian about all this, but I've barely seen him."

"If I see him, I'll tell him to catch up with you."

"Thanks. I miss talking to him."

"I bet he misses that too."

Eddy walks Max out and then keeps moving down the hall to Adrian's room. He knocks on the door and calls out his name. With no answer, he knocks again. He opens the door to be sure, and Adrian is not inside.

Eddy sighs and closes the door. The Neons are one of the worst gangs in Maiden City. *There's no way we can let them take Max back. He was so brave to leave in the first place.*

Eddy takes in the commotion of the halls and everything blurs. He shakes his head until he sees straight.

We can't let things go on like this.

Eddy promised to not let another kid go unnoticed to the point they do something reckless and hurt themselves. The images of DJ flipping out in the dining room those few weeks back shutter through his mind. The shelter closing left Eddy stressed, and he didn't listen carefully enough to DJ.

He frowns and moves up the hall. He'd take Max back to his place if he could see it being safer for him. *Who knows who's inside the shelter right now?* He certainly couldn't keep track of all the faces.

He moves into the donations room and finds Gene hanging up some clothes.

"Have you seen Jazz?" he asks.

"Not since this morning," Gene replies. "I've barely seen you all day."

"I got in late. Oh, do you have any spare pyjamas here?"

Gene looks over his shoulder at him. "For you?"

He shakes his head. "A girl."

Gene's eyebrows rise.

"Gene," Eddy lowers his tone. "I've got like five people I need to see at once. Do you have something or not?"

"Fine," Gene says, moving to the folded clothes and hands Eddy a t-shirt and shorts. "These should work."

"Thanks. Sorry for snapping."

"Don't mention it," Gene replies. "I've been waiting for your rubber band to snap. I reckon that still wasn't it."

Eddy smirks as he turns to leave. "Don't worry. I won't burst anytime soon." He swivels back to Gene to ask, "Have you talked to Max lately?"

Gene shrugs. "Not really. He's been different since Ferg left."

"You two aren't friends anymore?"

"We didn't have a fight or anything," Gene says. "We just don't hang out. He's not that easy to talk to anymore."

Eddy nods. "Ok. Thanks." He lifts the clothes. "And thanks, again."

It was weird not seeing Adrian all day. They usually see each other at least once, but this whole week has been crazy. Barely a moment to breathe.

His first real breath in hours comes when he unlocks the door to his apartment. The thought of seeing her beautiful face got him through a gruelling day.

"Aria," he calls out. "It's just me. Eddy."

He walks through the apartment, careful not to startle her if she wasn't in the bedroom resting.

"I'm sorry," her voice calls back, it's shaky and at a higher pitch.

"Sorry?"

He walks to the kitchen and finds her crouched on the tiles, trying to clean up broken glass. Streaks of red swirl with water along the patterned tiles.

"What happened?" he asks with alarm, making his way to her. "Are you hurt?"

"I dropped it," she says, her hair covering her face as head stays down. Her hands sweep at the smashed glass. "I tried to clean it up before you got back."

"Aria, stop," he says gently, grasping her wrist. "Stop, you're cutting yourself."

Two sobs tumble out of her. "Sorry. I didn't know what to do."

"Don't be sorry. It's ok. It was an accident." He cups her hands, keeping her palms upright. "You shouldn't be on the floor. Your ankle must be killing you. I'll help you up."

She nods, keeping her head down.

Eddy leans close to her. "Put your arms around my neck. I'm

going to lift you up. Ok?"

She puts her arms around him and nods against the nape of his neck.

Eddy holds her by the waist and counts aloud to three. A squeak whimpers out of her as they stand.

"Lean on me," he whispers. "Don't put pressure on your foot."

"I'm ok," she says. "I'm so stupid."

"No, you're not." He keeps a hold of her as they stand. "I'm going to sit you on the bench. Ok?"

"Ok."

He pulls her close and lifts her onto the bench. He then pulls a stool out and props her broken ankle on top of it.

"Comfy?"

She displays a limp smile as she holds up her bloodied palms. "Yes."

Eddy retrieves his first aid kit from the bathroom. He gently wipes Aria's hands with a cloth and then picks up the tweezers.

"This might sting."

"I'll be ok. Compared to the foot, I'm sure I can handle it."

Eddy smiles and studies her hand closely to find small pieces of glass lodged in her skin. "You're one strong woman."

"I've never thought of myself as strong."

Eddy finds a small piece of glass embedded in a line of her palm. He squeezes the back of her hand as he pulls at the piece with the tweezers. A hiss slithers out of Aria as it's yanked from her skin.

"Got it," he whispers.

"Ouch," she says with a smile. "Thank you."

He brushes a finger over her palm. "I think that's it for this hand. Do you feel anything?"

"They both sting, so I dunno."

"It doesn't look like there's anything. Are you ready for the next one?"

"No, but go for it."

He smiles. "Ok."

"Mamma does all the cleaning at home," she says. "I couldn't think how to clean it up. I panicked."

"That's ok," he says, inspecting her other hand. "You could have just left it. I would have been ok with cleaning it up once I got home."

"I felt bad. It looked very expensive."

He looks up and finds her eyes. They are red and tired. "Remember, none of this stuff is mine. And my mother won't care about it. She left it all behind. I doubt she remembers what's in here."

"They don't visit?"

"I haven't seen them in a long time." The tweezers nick another piece of glass. "Found one. Ready?"

"Yank it."

"One, two, three..."

"Ouch!"

Eddy places his thumb over the spot he pulled the glass from and applies pleasure. "That was deep. It's bleeding a little. Sorry."

"Better out, I guess."

"Definitely."

"Thanks for helping me. I feel like I've been nothing but trouble."

"You're no trouble. I feel bad. I shouldn't have left you alone," he says, his heart aching. "Tomorrow I'll take you with me."

"I'm so sorry for being such a pain."

"You're not. You're really not. I shouldn't have abandoned you after such a big accident. I'm sorry for not being more thoughtful."

A half smile curls her lips. "You left me in a fancy palace, I wouldn't call that mean."

Eddy smiles. "I'm glad you like it here."

"I guess, I got scared... that's why I dropped the glass."

"You got scared? Like a noise, or something?"

Aria bites her lip and shakes her head. "My family. Thinking about my life with them made me angry. I think it's the anger that frightened me."

"You're safe here. I can help you get away from them. If that's what you want?"

"I can't believe I'm away from them. I've never been away from them."

"What have you always wanted to do, but felt like you never could when you were with them?"

Aria lets out a nervous laugh. "Too many things to list."

"There's one more little piece. You ready?"

"Yep. Do it."

Eddy counts to three, and then fishes the small piece of glass out of her palm.

"*Geez,*" she hisses. "That one hurt the most."

"You wouldn't know it," Eddy says, and scoops the pieces of glass in the bin. "You're brave."

"I just feel stupid."

He meets her hazel eyes and watches the brown flecks glimmer against the light. "Why do you call yourself that?"

Aria looks away, a pout to her lips as she shrugs. "I've heard it a lot. I think it's true."

Eddy lifts her chin with the crook of his index finger. "Don't believe it."

Aria's mouth drops as surprise brings a rosy hue to her cheeks.

Eddy drops his hand and moves to the sink. "I'll clean up your hands for you. And I'll put some rubbing alcohol on them. It might sting."

"They already sting. No big deal," Aria says. "How was work? I didn't realise there are so many homeless people in Maiden City."

Eddy wipes a damp cloth against her hands, and says, "This city is broken. Unfortunately, the wrong kind of people are overrunning the centre. They're using it as a place to hang out, but I'm worried they're using it to find or supply drugs."

"Can you tell the police?"

"I think they are the people who have the police in their back pocket."

Aria looks at him, confused.

"There's a lot of corruption in this city. You can't always rely on the authorities."

Aria's face falls. "Oh, really?"

"That's why we have the shelter, so we can help people." Eddy's lips twist as he looks to the side. "I'm glad I went in today. There were some people I needed to check in on. And there's one kid in particular I'm worried about."

"Want to talk about it?"

Eddy smiles at her, appreciative of the offer. "Thanks, but I can't talk about what anyone tells me in private."

"Oh, ok. Of course."

"But, you know, it will be the same with you. If you want to talk about anything, I won't tell another person."

Aria chews her lip, like she's worried about what her answer might be.

Eddy balls up the cloth and sticks a bandage over each of her palms. "They shouldn't bleed much, but this should make them feel better."

"You're a good doctor," Aria whispers.

"I brought home dinner, and I have something for you to wear at night. That's if you still want to stay here."

She nods. "Yes, please."

"Not a problem. You'll take my bed."

"No. I can't take your bed."

"You won't win the argument," Eddy says, grinning. "I'm taking the couch and you'll take the bed. You need a bed with your injured foot."

"My foot is fine," she says, biting her lip to hide her smile.

"You won't win," he says, letting a laugh escape him. "The bed is all yours."

"Ok." She giggles. "I'm pretty tired, anyway. It's been a long day."

Money

Aria pleaded her case but lost the fight. It made her laugh.

She and Eddy playfully argued about who would get the bed. Aria genuinely felt he should take it. It is his bed, after all. Eddy said he didn't want her being in anymore pain than she already was. He was happy with the couch and led her to the bedroom.

Lying in the heavenly soft bed, in the middle of the night, the darkness consumes her. When she closes her eyes, flashes of Valeria's attack shutter through her mind. She jolts in the bed, the memory feeling as real as the actual attack.

She flinches throughout the night, like she would any other. It was the same during her hospital stay. Programmed to be on edge, waiting for a Valeria attack. Never knowing when a blade could come at her face or body.

As she stares at the blackened ceiling, noises sound in the apartment. Her eyes dart to the door. Fear surges through her. Valeria breaking down the door floods her imagination.

Gripping the bedsheet, she pushes herself up to sitting. When her heartbeat stops blaring in her ears, she realises it's Eddy's footsteps. She smiles and lets out a sigh of relief.

Her body stays grounded to the bed. Her parents drilled into her from a young age that she was never to get up during the night. Even without a wink of sleep, even if she wanted water or the bathroom, she was to stay in her bed until dawn.

His footsteps continue to pace. She worries something might be wrong.

She carefully pulls her feet from the covers, and plants them on the ground. She makes her way over to the chair by the dresser where she left the sweatshirt Eddy lent her. She's grateful for the pyjamas he brought home for her, but secretly, she really loved being in his clothes. They smelt of sweet yet masculine cologne and there was a certain soft comfort to them.

She pulls on the sweatshirt and then, as quietly as she can, she makes her way to the door. She opens it with a creak and finds light coming from down the hall. She wishes she could tiptoe, but she manages a light scuff with her moon boot.

She passes the living room and finds a lit alcove with a small desk, and Eddy bent over it.

He turns and meets her eyes. "Oh, hi. Did I wake you?"

"No. I couldn't sleep."

"Hard in a new place?"

"It's not that. I never sleep."

"Oh, I'm sorry to hear that. I'm never usually this bad. Just the last few weeks, I've been too stressed. I can't turn off at night."

"Like your thoughts keep running?"

"Yeah. Is that what it's like for you?"

"A little. I'm just always on edge."

"Did something happen to you at night?"

Aria looks away, biting her lip, trying to think of a way to change the subject.

"Tea is good for getting back to sleep," Eddy says, like he didn't just ask the question. "I'll make us some tea. Do you like camomile?"

Aria's chest eases, glad for the subject switch. "Never had it before."

"Really? It's good for relaxing and it's calming. Will you try it?"

"Sure."

She follows him into the kitchen and enjoys watching him work his way around the cupboards. He pulls a box from one cupboard, a teapot from another, and then a teaspoon which he uses to take tea leaves from the box and into the teapot.

"It looks strange," Aria says.

He smirks. "Tea leaves do look weird. But once it's brewed, you get rid of the leaves and you're left with something nice to drink."

Aria sits on a stool by the bench. "We will see."

"How long have you had trouble sleeping?"

"The last few years. I get jumpy from small noises. Lots of things wake me up."

Eddy pours water into the teapot, and asks, "Do you ever dream things that wake you up?"

"Sometimes."

He takes the teapot to the stove and ignites the burner, and asks, "Did an event trigger your sleep problems?"

She tilts her head and narrows her eyes. "What do you mean?"

He turns from the stove and slings his hands into the pockets of his sweatpants. "Sometimes one event can make us feel bad for years. Do your dreams make you feel bad?"

Aria chews her lip and looks down to her hands as she picks at her fingernails. "I guess."

"Is it stress that keeps you awake at night?" Eddy swipes a hand over his hair and sighs. "Sorry. My therapy brain never switches off."

"Maybe you're the one that's stressed?"

"I know I am. But more than one of us can be stressed."

Tension builds between Aria's shoulders. She closes her eyes and inhales a large breath. The bruise on her shoulder pulsates, making her wince. "I feel like my family's all or nothing."

"How so?"

She opens her eyes, takes in his concerned frame, and exhales.

"They put all their money into making me a champion," she whispers. "Their banking on me bringing them happiness."

Eddy leans against the bench and looks to the side. "What kinds of things does your family do together besides swimming?"

Aria picks harder at a jagged nail. "Eat."

"No, other activities."

"Nothing since church."

Eddy finds her eyes again. "Your family stopped going to church?"

"Pa said it was a distraction."

"How so?"

"Anything that doesn't involve swimming is a distraction."

The teapot sings on the stove and plumes of white steam rise from the spout. Eddy pushes off the bench and removes the teapot from the stove, turning off the burner.

Aria sits taller as she watches Eddy pull cups from a cupboard and then pour tea into them. Memories of choir robes, wooden pews, stained glass windows, and her cousin Helen flash through her mind.

"I used to sing in church," she blurts.

Eddy sets the teapot down and smiles as he slides a cup towards her. "Oh, yeah?"

"I haven't been happy since Pappa banned me from church. Banned me from singing."

"A ban from singing at church? Or singing altogether?"

"I can't sing at home," Aria says, wrapping her hands around the cup. "It upsets Mamma."

"You haven't talked much about her," Eddy says, lifting his cup and steam dances off the top of it. "How does she feel about your swimming?"

"She wants me to be the best so we can go back to church."

Eddy places his cup back on the bench without taking a sip.

"I'm not making sense?" Aria whispers, embarrassed.

"No, you're ok," Eddy says, leaning against the bench again. "I don't know your family, so it's all new for me. Do you feel comfortable talking about all this?"

"Maybe if I get it off my chest it'll help me sleep?"

Eddy grins. "That would be my thinking."

Aria leans over her flowery tea, and asks, "How do I tell my parents I don't want to swim?"

"You're eighteen, right? You're an adult who can make your own decisions."

Aria pulls herself up. "I don't think so."

Eddy picks up his cup and takes a sip. He nods and says, "It can be tough telling your parents the truth. I know from experience."

Aria looks around the darkened, yet still sparkly from expensive items, room. "What happened between you and your parents? I can't imagine growing up with parents who have so much money they can abandon an apartment when they feel like it. Did you grow up getting anything you wanted?"

Eddy moves around the bench and sits on the stool beside Aria. "My parents don't have a lot of money. You know what debt is?"

"Like when you get money from the bank to buy things and you have to pay it back?"

"Yeah. That's how my parents live. They work overtime every day of the week, trying to accumulate money. They spend every cent they earn and they keep racking up debt."

"Oh." Aria's body shrinks. "That doesn't sound good. Does money stress you out?"

Eddy puts his hands up; a defeated look crosses his face. "I want nothing to do with money."

When Eddy places his hands on the bench, Aria pats one of his hands, feeling like he needs a show of support.

The corners of his lips curl up. "Thanks."

"How long since you've seen them?"

"Almost a year."

Aria takes her hand away. "I don't know if I could spend that long away from my family. Although, it's been years since I've seen my uncles, aunts and cousins. Maybe I could do it?"

"Did you only see them at church?"

"We used to have a lot of family gatherings. One big, long table with lots of food. Pastas, roast meats and vegetables, yummy desserts."

"I've never had a big family event like that."

"They were really fun," Aria says, catching herself smiling at the memory. "We'd meet up for all the big holidays. Shrove Tuesday, Easter Sunday, Christmas. Sometimes it'd just be Sunday dinner after church. We'd play games like charades and sing silly nursery rhymes. Times were good when he got on with his brothers." Aria laughs and adds, "I remember Pa had a pretty good singing voice."

"Really."

"He'd sing with me when we were at my grandparents' house. I remember thinking I had the greatest dad on the planet." Aria's smile disappears, and she looks to her hands as she picks at a nail. "Then it was like Pappa flicked a switch one day and it was all gone."

"That's rough. There was no explanation?"

"I didn't even get to say goodbye to people." Aria swallows hard. "One day I was in choir practice and he stomped his way through the church. Everyone stopped practicing and focused on him. He grabbed my arm and pulled me out of the group." She closes her eyes as it replays in her mind. "He yelled at me in front of everyone. He yelled that I couldn't be there. That it was betraying him."

Aria opens her eyes as she feels Eddy's hand rub her back.

"It was four years ago," she murmurs. "Feels long ago, but also like yesterday. I try not to think about it."

"It was four years ago we started the shelter. I know what you mean about it feeling like yesterday and an eternity ago."

"Your parents didn't approve?"

Eddy lets out an uncomfortable laugh. "No, they did not. They wanted me to continue with school to become a psychologist. I mean, I want that too, but there's nothing like the hands on experience I'm getting now. I can't shake the workaholic nature. That must be genetic."

"I'm looking forward to seeing your work tomorrow."

"Why did your father say you were betraying him?"

"Because Ma and I still went to church." She lets out a weighted breath. "We didn't think he was serious, like it was a joke. He took me home and then started yelling at Mamma that she shouldn't have let me go to practice. I feel bad for Ma. She's cut off from her friends too."

"Do you remember anything that led up to that?"

Aria pats her eyes dry and nods. "Yeah. He was having fights with his brothers."

"Physical fights?"

She shakes her head. "I don't think so. More like they would ridicule him."

"They embarrassed him?"

"Pa wants to prove himself as the greatest swimming coach in Maiden City. If I'm a winner, he can go back to his brothers and they will praise him. Then we can go back with acceptance."

"You just won a championship. Can't you go back now?"

"I've won championships before. I've won lots of time before."

"So, when is it enough?"

Aria raises her palms up, a tear rolling down her cheek. "When I'm champion of the world?"

"I'll help you however I can so you can tell them you want to stop swimming. They can't treat you like this. It's like you're a slave in the water."

A sad laugh puffs out of Aria. "Sometimes I look at my dad when I'm swimming a lap. He looks like he thinks he's king of the water. I thought maybe I'd be a princess, but slave makes more sense."

"I didn't mean to make you feel bad."

Aria presses her hand on top of his. "You didn't. It's good to say these things out loud, for once."

Eddy's pinky finger rubs against hers. "Your sister doesn't feel the same way?"

Aria moves her hand away. "No, she agrees with everything Pa says. She'd happily train all day and night if Pa wanted her too."

"He doesn't train you two the same?"

"No. She doesn't make good times. He forgets about her and concentrates on me. I hate that."

"You feel bad for your sister?"

She frowns and nods. "Yeah. It plays with my sister's mind. She's jealous of my achievements and it causes her to do bad things. She hides away in Pa's shed like it gives her the tools for survival."

"I'm sorry to hear you're both not coping at home."

"Valeria never wants to leave home. She knows I do and urged me to go."

"She's happy at home?"

"I dunno." Aria shrugs. "I don't know if anyone is happy. Pappa is doing all of this to make himself happy. He will cheer at the swimming pool for everyone to applaud me, but it's never enough."

"So, all this training is because he wants to prove himself by using you?" Eddy says. "It's his issue."

"I know it is."

"Don't let anyone say you are stupid," Eddy says, looking deeply into her eyes. "You are smart, Aria."

Aria swings her moon boot. "But now I have this thing stopping me."

"It's giving you time to gain the courage to tell your father you don't want to be in the water."

"I don't want to make it tough on them. They're already going to lose sponsorship money because I can't compete. All our money comes from me. All because someone once told Pa I was the best swimmer he'd seen in years. It was like Pappa had stars in his eyes. Then our lives changed."

Sadness clouds Eddy's eyes. He rubs his chin as he stares at her moon boot. "So, he didn't do that to you?"

Aria's mouth drops and she gasps. "No, never. He's devastated I'm not in the water."

"He seems so controlling, I thought he might have taken something out in anger." Eddy finds her eyes, and the sorrow hurts her. "Do you mind if I ask how it happened?"

Aria looks away from him, her eyes stinging with tears from his immense care. She looks at the boot and says, "Oh, it was just a silly accident. I tripped down the stairs." She adds a laugh to play it off. "Hurt like nothing I'd ever felt before."

"I'll bet." Eddy rubs her arm. "I'm sorry that happened to you."

Delightful goosebumps course her skin from his touch. She smiles and blushes as her heart patters.

"Thanks."

Eddy removes his hand and chews his lip. "Are you feeling sleepier?"

Aria lifts her cup, realising she hadn't tried the tea. She takes a sip, and the taste slides over her tongue. Not sweet, not bitter, not bad.

She places the cup down. "I don't know about sleepy, but better, I think. Relieved?"

"It's always good to have someone to talk to."

Aria's blush turns up a notch. "I hope you felt better talking to me, too."

He smiles and looks through her eyes to her soul. "I did. I don't talk about myself that much. It was nice."

"I'm glad."

Tagged

Aria's eyes bug as she takes in the crowd of people in the shelter. The noise buzzes at her ears and she can hardly think.

She follows closely behind Eddy, who zigzags around people. Some are dirty and hunched, fear clouding their eyes. Others stand tall in loud groups. Perfect teeth and well-tailored clothing.

The clash makes Aria dizzy.

"Eddy," a woman calls over the noise as she rushes towards them. Her beauty leaves Aria breathless. Her hair has the shine of moonlight bouncing off a midnight sky. Her skin is silky like caramel, and her body is lean and toned like a supermodel.

"Where have you been?" the woman asks frantically.

"Sorry," Eddy says, stepping out of the way of a pair of guys laughing and taking up the hallway. "Where's Adrian?"

"Common room," she replies, throwing a thumb over her shoulder. "Have you—"

"—This is Aria," Eddy introduces, cutting her off. "Can you look after her?"

"Oh," she says, looking at Aria for the first time. "Hi, sorry, I didn't see you there."

Aria glances at their surroundings and then back to her. "It's wild in here."

The woman blows out a breath. "Yeah, I know."

"You're good?" Eddy says to the woman, taking a step forward.

"You're going?" Aria blurts, reaching for him.

Eddy whips around, finding her eyes with concern. "Sorry, I need to check on some people." He glances at the beauty beside him and then back to Aria. "This is Jazz, she'll show you around. Jazz, you'll stay with her?"

"Yes, sure," Jazz replies.

Eddy squeezes Aria's hand. "I'll come back and find you. If you need me, let Jazz know and she can bring you to my office. Ok?"

Aria nods. "Ok."

Eddy smiles and drops her hand, and leaves down the hall.

"You go to MCU?" Jazz asks, pointing to the Maiden City University sweatshirt Aria is wearing.

"Oh," Aria says, pulling at the shirt. "No, it's Eddy's."

"Do you want a change of clothes? We have plenty here."

"I don't mind."

"Come, I'll show you," Jazz says, starting them off down the hall. "I graduated from MCU this year. It's a good university, if it's something you're interested in."

"I wouldn't know what to study," Aria says, leaving her lack of a high school education out of the equation.

"Yeah, there is a lot of choice. It's hard to know if you're following the right path, or someone else's. How do you know Eddy?"

Aria leaves it vague with, "We swim at the same pool."

"Oh, ok." Jazz leads her to a room, and says, "Here we are."

Aria looks into the room to find racks of neatly colour-coded hanging clothes. "Wow."

"Gene is very particular about sorting the clothes."

"You didn't want to see the state of this place before I got here," a voice answers from behind the clothes. A boy rounds the rack, a mess of dark curls atop his head, and a sheer navy scarf tied around his neck. "Oh, hey there."

"Gene, this is Aria," Jazz introduces. "Do you have something for her?"

"My God, you're spectacular," Gene says, pacing towards Aria. "That hair."

"Huh?" Aria hunches as Gene picks up a lock of her hair.

"*Gene*," Jazz says, tapping his hand. "Let her go. She just got here."

Gene takes a step back. "I'm sorry, but you look like a princess or something."

Aria splutters a laugh. "Me?"

"Peachy, rosy skin and hair like golden copper," Gene says, staring at her in awe.

Jazz laughs and spins him around. "Just find some clothes. You just called her skin and hair two totally different colours in the one sentence."

"Well, do you not see it?" Gene says, thumbing through the rack of bright colours. "Trust me, I'm dead on. She's perfection."

"Oh hush," Jazz says. "Sorry Aria, if he's making you feel uncomfortable."

Aria fans her face. "It's ok. That's probably more compliments than I've ever gotten in my life combined."

"Not possible," Gene mutters, studying the clothes.

"*Gene*," Jazz hisses. "Stop it." She leans into him and whispers, "You don't know where she's come from. Cool it."

Aria steps closer to them, waving her hands. "No, it's ok. I'm not damaged or anything."

Gene turns around and waggles a finger at her moon boot. "And what's this all about?"

"*Gene*," Jazz snaps, aggravated.

"It's ok," Aria hurries. "I fell and broke my ankle. That's all."

"Oh, no biggy," Gene says sarcastically. "A broken ankle is a big deal, girl."

"You don't have to give us any details," Jazz says to her, firm yet sweet. "Eddy told you he's a counsellor?"

Aria nods. "Yes, we've talked about that."

"Oh, that's where he's been," Gene drags out the words. He pulls out a vibrant green summer dress with a daisy pattern lining the waist and bottom hem. "Oh, is this perfect or what."

"That's too cute," Jazz says. "Geez, they didn't have cute stuff like this when I needed clothes." She turns to Aria. "Do you like it?"

"It's lovely. I'm just not sure it's me."

"*Pfft*." Gene holds the dress up against Aria. "It's one-hundred percent your colour."

"It's shorter that I would normally wear," Aria mutters nervously.

"Get her something longer," Jazz orders quickly.

Gene turns back to the rack, but Aria stops him. "No, it's ok," she says, hand out for the dress. "I'd like to try it. If that's ok?"

Gene turns around, light dancing in his dark brown eyes. "More than ok. Get it, girl."

When Aria takes the dress from Gene, a ringtone beeps. Jazz pulls her phone from her pocket and her eyes round as she looks at the screen.

Jazz lifts her index finger and says to them, "I've got to take this."

She backs out of the room and answers the call.

"I don't know where she thinks she can go to hear the other person on the call," Gene says with a light eye roll.

"It's very crowded out there," Aria replies.

"Tell me about it. They haven't taken over this room yet. And I tell you, if I come in here and find it trashed, I'm gonna lose it."

"All these clothes are yours?"

Gene smirks. "I just organise them. They're for everyone. But when anyone else is in charge of this room, it looks like an explosion."

"You live here? Or work here?"

"Both," he says with a shrug. He looks at Aria, tilting his head. "You look familiar."

Aria smiles with surprise and touches her hair. "I do?"

"Did you go to Walsh High School?"

"No, the Catholic school."

"The one in Hamlet? I must have seen you around the neighbourhood."

"Maybe. I don't go out much."

"Are your parents strict?" Gene asks. "My dad is a hard-ass too. I'm so glad to be out of home."

Aria leans against a clothing rack and whispers, "What did he do?"

Gene steps closer to Aria and whispers, "He'd hit me."

A gasp flies out of her. She covers her mouth and muffles, "I'm sorry."

"Don't be. I'm out now." Gene nods to her encased foot. "Who did that to you?"

Aria steps back. "No one."

"You can say, you know. It's safe here. They'll help you."

"It was an accident," Aria says as hurriedly as the beating of her heart. "I tripped."

Gene lifts his hands in defence. "Ok, whatever you say. Did Eddy help you here?"

"Yeah, he helped me get away from home." A nervous laugh trickles out of her. "Last night was the first time I didn't sleep in my own bed."

Gene's eyes slit as his head tilts. "You were at Eddy's house?"

She chews her lip. "Yeah."

"You're the girl he got pyjamas for?"

"I guess."

Gene laughs, pressing into his stomach. "That's fantastic. Eddy needs to let off some steam."

Aria's stomach flips. She backs away from him, a sour taste lining the back of her mouth.

"I wasn't trying to say you guys were doing anything," Gene is quick to backtrack.

"You think I'm immoral?" she asks in a timid voice.

"Immoral? We got a lot worse under this roof than a Catholic schoolgirl."

"I dropped out of school at fourteen."

"You don't look like a bad girl," Gene says, a kindness to his tone. "You look scared."

Aria frowns. "I do?"

He smiles. "But we all are."

Aria looks back at the door. "Even Jazz?"

"You know who she is, right?"

"A supermodel?"

"Close. She's Jazz Abadi from Ultimate ME."

"The gym?"

"Yeah."

Aria grins, shaking her head. "I think I've met her before."

"Huh? When?"

"I won a short pass to one of their gyms. There was this media photo opp, thing. I'm pretty sure she was there."

Gene pulls out his phone. "Oh, that's why you look familiar." He scrolls on his phone and then turns the screen to Aria. "This is you."

Aria's eyes enlarge as she looks at herself next to Jazz on his phone. "Yeah, that was the day. How do you have the photo?"

"It's on Jazz's Collage account. You're not tagged."

"Tagged?"

"Your account isn't connected with the photo."

"I don't have an account."

"Good lord. You're in the dark ages like Adrian. At least tell me you have a phone."

Aria shakes her head. "I've never needed one."

"Those words don't even make sense to me," Gene jokes.

"My dad takes me and my sister wherever we need to go, and we have a landline at home."

"Yep, dark ages."

Aria blushes as she giggles.

"So, how come you and Jazz both didn't recognise each other?" Gene asks.

"The photo makes it look friendlier than it was. She was super busy."

"Yeah, she's a bit of a control freak."

"The bigger question is, how did you remember me from one photo?"

"For one, when I was home and miserable, I'd study everything Jazz did. *Super fan*. It was better than thinking about my own crummy life. And two, I don't think it was just the picture. It's the hair. I'm sure I've fanboyed over it in my neighbourhood."

Aria combs her fingers through her hair. "It is a vibrant colour."

"An unforgettable colour."

Burden

Eddy grabs a hold of Adrian as soon as he sees him in the hall. "Can I talk to you?"

"Right now?" Adrian asks, exhaustion dulling his eyes.

Eddy rocks his jaw and nods at the people milling around them. "Right. You're busy. I'm busy. Right."

Adrian's eyes narrow. "Ed? What's wrong? You seem scattered."

Eddy takes a step away. "Nah, it's ok. Don't worry."

Adrian spins Eddy around and pushes him up the hall. "C'mon. I can spare ten minutes for you."

They go into Adrian's room and Eddy paces by the desk.

"What's up?" Adrian asks. "Is it all the people? Are you too stressed out? I don't think I could handle you falling apart."

"No. It's this girl," Eddy says, chewing on a fingernail. "She needed help, and I didn't think she could handle the noise."

"Someone who needs to be here?" Adrian says with concern. "Where is she now?"

"She's here now," Eddy says, a swirl of guilt flowing through his stomach.

"Oh, ok. Well, good. It's crowded here, but we still help those who need it. Want me to talk to her?"

"Jazz is with her."

"Ok, good. Hey, what's up with you?"

Eddy looks to his shoes. "What?"

"You're acting so weird. What's wrong? Did something messed up happen with her?"

Eddy rubs the back of his neck, and his clammy palm slides over the beads of sweat.

"Ed?"

"I think I did something stupid," Eddy whispers.

Adrian's eyes widen, and he slowly sits on the desk. "What did you do?"

"I took her to my apartment instead of coming straight here."

"Oh." Adrian pauses, glancing down, back to Eddy, and down again. "And why did you do that?"

"That's what I'm afraid of," Eddy says. "That I did it because I'm attracted to her. I put that above helping her."

"But you helped her," Adrian says. "Right?"

"Well, yeah."

"Did anything romantic happen?"

"Not really, but I couldn't stop thinking about how beautiful she is."

"You are human, Ed."

"I'm also a counsellor first."

"She's not your patient. You're allowed to be attracted to someone."

"I dunno. I saw her in trouble and that should have been my number one priority."

"Wait, you didn't act on helping her right away because you were too busy with a crush?"

Eddy rubs his chin. "No, I got to her in time."

"So, it didn't stop you from helping her?"

"I paid attention to what was going on around her. With her family and her demeanour."

Adrian slides off the desk and laughs. "Doesn't sound like you did anything wrong."

"But she slept in my bed," Eddy blurts, refusing to ease his guilt.

Adrian deadpans. "You slept with her?"

Eddy gasps. "No way. I slept on the couch."

"Then why are you torturing yourself?"

Eddy exhales and slumps in the chair. "I like her too much. She's always in my thoughts." He meets Adrian's eyes and says, "And her voice. Ah, you should hear her sing."

Adrian smiles. "Really?"

"Like an angel."

The door pushes open, and Jazz steps in with her phone glued to her ear. She looks at them both, and then backs out of the room, shutting the door.

"Jazz?" Adrian calls, moving towards the door.

"She's supposed to be with Aria," Eddy says, frustrated.

Adrian opens the door and steps into the hall. He looks back at Eddy and asks, "Are you ok?"

"Yeah. I'm going to check on Aria."

"Ok. Find me later. I want to find Jazz and see what that was all about."

Adrian is quick down the hall, weaving between people as he chases Jazz.

Eddy peers down both ends of the hall, trying to work out where Aria might be. He moves toward the dining hall, when Max barges past him.

"*Whoah*, where are you going?" Eddy asks, reaching for Max.

"Nowhere," Max mutters, pushing forward.

"Hey. Wait up," Eddy says, spinning to chase Max.

"No. I need to get outta here."

"Where are you going?"

"Just out. I can't stand it in here."

"You're coming back, though?"

Max groans. "I dunno. Ferg just upped and left one day. Maybe I should just do the same."

"You said you trusted us to fix it."

"I can't wait for however long that will take."

"Give us more than a day."

"Is Adrian even going to fix it? Does he care? Or does he only care about what his girlfriend says?"

"I was just with Adrian. I'll get him for you."

"Leave me alone, Ed. I need some time alone."

Eddy stops and drops his hands to his sides. "Ok then."

With a thudding heart, Eddy turns towards the dining room. He passes his office to see the door open with a girl standing in the doorway.

"Oh, good, you're here," Tessa says with an eager smile.

"Huh?" Eddy replies, his head a jumble of thoughts.

Tessa looks back at his desk and then back to Eddy. "We had a time booked in now to sit down and chat."

"Oh crap," Eddy whispers. "Sorry, I forgot. Um..." He tries to think of an excuse to cancel or push back the session. He looks at her fear-soaked eyes, and another layer of guilt builds inside him. "Let's go inside. Shall we?"

Hope brightens her face. She nods and turns into his office.

Eddy rubs his heart, hoping Aria is ok and not overwhelmed in the chaotic shelter.

"I found a place I can move into," Tessa says when Eddy closes the door behind them.

"Really? That's great. Where is it?"

Hesitation twitches Tessa's eyebrows, and she blows out a breath. "This guy has a room to rent. It's a small flat above a nightclub."

Eddy frowns. "It's in the Nightclub District?"

Tessa hugs her small frame. "I was worried about taking up room when this place was out of money. How can I stay when there's so many people? I don't want to burden you guys any longer."

"You're not leaving," Eddy says, firm yet kind. "This is outrageous. We can't have you living in a dump with some creep."

"I didn't say—"

"—You didn't have to," Eddy cuts her off. "Your body language told me everything. I'm not letting you put yourself in harm's way. People come here from places in the Nightclub District or The Limits. I'm going to talk to Jazz and put an end to this craziness."

"Don't get her mad," Tessa pleads. "She might be over-the-top, but I don't want her to go."

"She won't leave. She just needs to slow down."

"I didn't mean to upset you."

"You didn't. I'm sorry, I didn't mean to come across so brash. I'm already preoccupied."

"I should go and give you some time to think."

"No, don't go. I'm here for you."

Tessa smiles kindly on him. "I'm being here for you. Keep the door shut and be in the quiet for ten minutes."

Eddy flops in his chair, grateful for her kindness. "Only if you promise not to move out."

"I'll stay until I find a better place."

"Deal."

Tessa leaves the room and Eddy rubs the sharp pain in his forehead.

He stands, wanting to find Aria. His mind thrashes with thoughts of Max. *Where would he have gone to? I should find him first. But I don't know if Aria is ok, or if she's alone.*

He sits down, his head spinning. He rubs his temples, scrunching his eyes closed. Panic rises inside him, and he fights back, trying to be still and clear his mind.

We can't have people like Tessa fleeing the shelter because they don't feel welcome anymore. He doesn't want anyone feeling like a burden and getting themselves into trouble. *I need to talk to Jazz.*

His stomach churns, and he questions whether he has any right to bring it up with Jazz.

She's trying her best, and she's completely new to this. She didn't want all these people to flood this place.

Eddy doesn't want to make things any harder for Adrian either. He's watched the pair become icy when they disagree on her marketing efforts for the shelter.

I don't want to make things worse.

But can they get worse than this?

Advantage

Adrian's back knots. He hates fighting with Jazz, but it keeps happening.

"Why won't you let me help you?" he asks her, trying to keep his cool.

"We're both working to keep this place running," Jazz replies, "but does that mean we need to work *together*? Can't we work separately on projects to get to the same goal?"

"This isn't like your old job, Jazz."

Jazz groans and turns her back on him, her fingers flexing by her sides. "I'm aware."

Adrian steps close to her, running his hand along her back. "Why won't you talk to me?"

She flinches. "What? So, you can yell at me again?"

He steps away, frowning. "I said I was sorry about that."

"I know," she says with a cold edge.

"You don't believe me?"

"I didn't say that."

"Who was on the phone?"

"No one."

"We're s'pose to be in a relationship." He rubs his constricted chest. "We should be able to talk better than this."

She finds his eyes, and Adrian notes the sadness rounding them. "I guess you're better at the talking than me."

He reaches for her hand. "Don't be like that."

Jazz looks at his hand, and hesitation etches her face. She sniffs and takes his hand. She steps in close, and he wraps his other arm around her. She shivers and rests her head against his shoulder.

"You don't need to stress yourself out so much," he whispers by her ear.

"Look at the mess I made," she whispers into his shirt.

He strokes her hair. "You didn't mean for it to get this out of hand. I know you didn't."

"I didn't think people would take advantage."

"Maybe some of them genuinely need our help."

"I hope not. I need to find Myra."

"That's not what we do. We help those who come to us. We don't go hunting for people."

Jazz pulls away. "She did come to us. I let her down."

"There's a reason she's running. Let her run. She knows where we are. She'll come back if it's safe."

"*If?*" Jazz says, backing away. "I can't wait for *if*. Time won't wait for *if*."

"Jazz," Adrian says, defeated, as she's already moving down the hall.

He leans against the wall and sinks his head into his hands. There's been an uncomfortable distance between him and Jazz for days. She finally lets her guard down, and he lets it fall the way of another argument.

I have to find the locket.

He's sure she's still holding a grudge against him for the part he played in the robbery of her family home when they were kids.

If I find the locket, maybe she'll open up to me. Trust me with her thoughts and let me help.

Adrian clenches his jaw. He has no idea how to locate the jewellery after all this time. He considers the internet might help, but he doesn't have the basic skills to navigate it. He makes his way to the donated clothes to ask Gene for help with the search.

Adrian opens the door and finds Gene sitting and talking with a girl with the brightest and silkiest red hair he's ever seen.

"Sorry, I should have knocked," Adrian says.

"It's cool," Gene says. "Have you two met? This is Aria."

"Oh, you're Aria," Adrian says, more enthusiastic than he meant to sound. He's very excited about his best friend having a crush. He wants to know more about this new girl.

Surprise fills Aria's eyes. "Yes, that's me."

"I'm Adrian." He slings his hands in the pockets of his jeans. "How are you doing?"

"I'm ok."

His enthusiasm drops as he notices the brace around her foot. He gestures to it, and asks, "That thing giving you any trouble?"

"Just the fact that it's there is annoying," Aria says. "At least it's keeping my foot in one piece."

"Did you break your ankle?"

"Yeah. It was a nasty break."

"It's good you could get it fixed. Most people here can't afford to go to the hospital."

"Pappa wouldn't let my foot go untreated."

Adrian's face brightens with curiosity. "You're close with your family?"

"They're the only people in my life." Her smile fades and her shoulders droop. "Until I left."

"It's ok to leave when you have to," Adrian says. "Plenty of us have issues with our families. Gene, did you talk to her about yours?"

Gene nods. "We come from the same neighbourhood."

"Maybe you two should stick together," Adrian suggests. "If you have things in common."

Gene smiles at Aria. "I don't mind."

"As long as you still do your homework," Adrian adds.

Gene groans. "Geez, is that all you came in here for?"

"I was gonna ask..." Adrian shakes his head and doesn't finish the sentence. He turns to Aria, and says, "I was talking to Eddy earlier, and just wanted to check that you were settling in ok."

"Oh," she replies. "Yeah, I'm fine."

"You wanna hang with me?" Gene asks.

Aria clasps her hands in front and bites her lip. She turns to Adrian as if asking for permission.

"You don't have to, if you don't want to. I can show you to a bed if you want to rest for a while," Adrian says, trying to resist staring at her moon boot. "You can do whatever you want."

A half smile dashes her lips, and she gives a quick shake of the head. "Whatever I want? That sounds wrong."

"No, really," Adrian insists. "You can stay as long as you want and leave whenever you want."

"But I hope you don't leave right away," Gene says to her.

Aria's smile renews Adrian's energy after his downward spiral with Jazz. He says goodbye to them and decides to interact with more people, in need of help, to keep his spirits up.

Magnetic

Aria's mind thrashes with images of her sister. The wild hate in her eyes. The crude weapons under her bed. The hammer she swung over her head.

She snaps out of her thoughts with violent gasps. Her hand presses on her leaping chest as her blood runs cold.

"Are you ok?" Jazz asks, standing in front of her in the dining room.

Aria shows Jazz a smile she hopes is believable. "Yes. Thanks. I'm ok."

Jazz smiles back and hands her a plate. "Hope you're hungry."

"Thanks," Aria says, taking the plate and letting Jazz fill it with food.

"Follow me," Gene says, nodding towards the tables, holding his own plate of food.

Aria follows him and they land at a table with two other people sitting at it.

Gene slides his textbook and notebook out from under his arm and lets them flop onto the table as he places his plate down.

"Jazz looks weird serving food," Aria says, watching Jazz's

graceful movements and the way her chin lifts as she smiles with pearly white teeth.

"Whatcha mean?" Gene asks, flipping through his book.

"The other people giving out the food look like they belong here, but Jazz... I dunno. Like... she's too perfect?"

"Well, yeah. She is perfection."

Aria giggles. "I forgot I was sitting with her number one fan."

Gene twirls his pen and nods at Jazz. "You're right, though. She is out of place here. But it weirdly works."

"She looks like she loves it here. But also, she's kinda distracted."

"I reckon she's feeling guilty."

"Guilty? Why?"

"Because she invited all these people in," Gene says, waving his pen at the crowd in the dining room. "She did a TV interview and people twisted her words. She said everyone was welcome, that even the rich could be anonymous. No questions asked."

"Seems pretty clear to me."

"What she meant was when she first came here, no one knew who she was even though she's rich and famous. She meant that it's safe here." Gene frowns as he looks at all the well-dressed, clean people. "They're all using this place as a hiding place to do shady stuff."

"Shady stuff?"

"They want a place the cops aren't hanging around. Not that it matters when so many can just pay them off."

Aria frowns. "They're just taking advantage of nice people. Makes me feel bad for being here."

"Don't be. Don't give these fools the satisfaction."

"Eddy told me there were lots of people here. It still didn't prepare me."

"Does it make you anxious?"

She breathes out slowly, and then says, "I'm not really used to people in general. The most crowded places I go to are swimming competitions, but I always have to sit with my family, and I don't socialise with any of the competitors. Except for my sister."

Aria's appetite diminishes as she takes in the faces. Anger wells inside her. The people running this place are making a safe haven for those who have nothing. How could people who don't need the help take up the space?

When she tries the food, a magnetic hum starts under her skin. She looks up and smiles before seeing him. Her auburn hair swings over her shoulder and Eddy walks into the room. There's a steady rhythm to her heartbeat, and she bites into her half smile.

Her hand lifts to wave, when someone else grabs Eddy's attention. She lowers her hand, and her smile slips away.

Seriousness overtakes Eddy's expression. His tired eyes take in the person talking to him, and then he nods. He follows the person through the crowd and they disappear into the kitchen.

"He'll never say no," Gene says.

Aria jumps, for a moment forgetting he was there. "Huh?"

"Eddy," Gene explains. "He'll never say no to anyone. If someone asks for help, he'll stop everything to help them."

"That's so kind."

"It'd be exhausting."

Aria sits back in her chair and sighs. "Yeah. He looks tired."

Guilt swells inside her. *I asked him to help, and he dropped everything to help me. He already had so many people asking things of him, and I've made it worse.*

"Except for yesterday," Gene says, tapping the pen to his lips as his eyes gaze upward in thought.

"Yesterday?"

"He zipped around here. Cut sessions short. Didn't talk to as many people in the halls. Like he was eager to get home."

A shy smile plays at her lips. "Really?"

"How are you guys going?" Adrian asks, sitting down at their table.

"I was just telling Aria about Eddy being a workaholic." Gene nudges Aria. "But this guy takes the cake for being a workaholic."

"Me?" Adrian says, stabbing at salad on his plate. "Nah, I don't work." He smiles at Aria. "No one pays me."

Gene laughs and flips a page of his book.

"How's your homework going?" Adrian asks him.

"Boring but fine."

"Teach me something," Adrian asks as he eats.

"Why don't you take a class?"

"Because I prefer you to teach me something. Proves you're studying."

"I could make it up for all you know."

Adrian smirks. "You wouldn't."

"I'd love to learn something too," Aria pipes up. "What subject are you studying?"

Gene shows her the cover. "Ancient Roman history. Oh, here's something I bet you didn't know. Ancient Romans used to wash their clothes in urine."

"*Eww*," Aria squeaks.

"That's made up," Adrian laughs.

"No, I'm dead serious." He slides the book to Aria and points to a line. "Can you read that?"

Aria reads the paragraph and laughs, pushing the book away. "*Eww*. That would have smelt so bad. Show Adrian."

Gene takes the book back. "Nah, Adrian doesn't do books. But maybe if I keep telling you guys gross things, you won't ask me to teach anything."

"Not gonna happen," Adrian says, smiling.

"I agree," Aria says. "I feel like there is a lot more of the world I have to know about."

"Well, that backfired then," Gene says, flipping another page.

"Do you still go to Walsh High?" Aria asks.

"No, I do classes online," Gene replies.

"You can do that?" Aria asks, intrigued.

Adrian looks over his shoulder and groans. "I'd better get to the kitchen and help. Where are all these people coming from?"

"Aid, just sit and eat. You're running on empty," Gene says.

"Not if they need help in there."

"I bet you anything Hector is eating while cooking," Gene says. "And besides, Eddy went in there to help."

Adrian turns back to his plate, relaxed. "Oh, did he?"

"Yeah, so just finish eating before you tornado around the place."

He picks up his fork. "Only if you teach us another fun fact."

"Nothing with bodily fluids," Aria jokes.

"Damn, that's my specialty," Gene says with a wink. "How about the gods they worshipped?"

"More than one?" Adrian asks.

Gene scans the page as he replies, "Did you know, the planets are named after Roman Gods? Like Jupiter, the god of the sky, Pluto, the god of the dead, and Neptune, the god of the sea."

"I kinda remember something about that from school," Aria says, memories of the classroom coming back to her. "I always liked Neptune. Something about him. Must be the water connection."

Gene reads over more Ancient Rome facts while they eat their dinner. Aria catches half of them as the noise around the tables increases in volume. Her head pulsates and thinking becomes difficult.

Adrian shifts in his chair, looking over his shoulder at distinct groups of people. Aria notes the concern on his face, and the way his eyes thoughtfully narrow.

Aria follows his eyes and searches the room. She flinches when her brain plays tricks. Valeria pops up between groups of people.

She gulps and her eyes flick to the kitchen door.

A hum plays under her skin and the kitchen door opens. Her

stomach jitters with butterflies as Eddy exits the kitchen.

Her smile is instant. Her heart bangs in her chest as she waits for his eyes to find hers. Anxiety squirms through her when it looks like someone else will gain his attention first. Eddy steps around a group of people and lands in her path.

His eyes enliven when they meet hers. She sits taller and the pounding of her heart accelerates.

Adrian and Gene look from Aria to Eddy and watch him approach the table.

Eddy pulls out the chair beside Adrian and sits across from Aria. "How are you?" he asks her.

"I'm ok. How are you?"

His smile drags to the left. "Better."

Tingles shoot from her heart and invigorate all her veins. Her temperature spikes when she realises Adrian and Gene are staring at them.

"Do they need help in the kitchen?" Adrian asks Eddy.

Eddy nods, rubbing behind his neck. "Yeah, it's a bit of a mess. They're starting on cleaning. I would have stayed in there, but I need to get back to my office." He turns back to Aria. "Just wanted to check on you."

Aria grins, her giddiness overriding her embarrassment.

"Maybe you should stay here for the night," Eddy suggests. "I'm going to be working late. There's too much going on for me to leave, and I don't want you waiting for me. I'd prefer you'd have a bed and get some rest."

"Ok," Aria says. "But I don't mind waiting. I don't really sleep, anyway."

"Maybe just snag a bed in case you get sleepy."

Aria nods.

"I'll show you where you can crash," Adrian tells her.

"Thank you," Eddy says to Adrian as he stands. He slides his chair under the table and his jaw rocks as he looks at Aria. "I'll try to catch you later."

She nods, hating seeing him so worn out.

Eddy drags himself away from the table towards the hall.

Adrian taps Gene's book and leans in close to whisper, "Does he seem different to you? He doesn't usually seem so unhappy to work."

"Well, this place isn't exactly normal right now," Gene murmurs.

Adrian looks to Aria, and she flinches in her seat, afraid she'll get scolded for eavesdropping.

"Sorry you came here when the place is so overcrowded," Adrian says to her. "It wasn't exactly what we had in mind."

"What did this place used to look like?" Aria asks, curious about what they all miss.

"Barren," Gene jokes.

"We were seconds from being shut down," Adrian says, "but all this is extreme. We need a good balance again. We used to know who everyone was, and you could hear yourself think. Now it's hard to judge who needs attention first."

"It's kinda easy," Gene says. "People who need help are like Aria. They sit down and talk to us. The people who give us shifty eyes and avoid talking are here for the wrong reasons."

"That's unfair," Adrian argues.

"You want to help everyone, regardless of money," Aria says, liking Adrian more and more.

"Yeah. I mean, maybe some of them came for a hide-out or a party place," Adrian says, "but what if they're just following a leader? What if they really need help? To get away from that person?"

Gene groans. "So, you agree with Jazz?"

"We go about it in different ways, but yes, we're on the same page."

Aria admires the purpose in Adrian's eyes. A sense of purpose she longs to have. "It sounds really nice. You make this place really welcoming."

He smiles. "Good to hear when you're seeing it like this."

"You'll turn it around," Aria says, somehow knowing her faith in him will ring true.

Permission

Aria misses him. She'd only spent one night at Eddy's apartment, but not seeing him now feels like torture. Made worse by the fact they are under the same roof. The crowds make them seem worlds apart.

She sits on the bottom bunk in a dorm-style room Adrian had shown her too. She picks at her fingernails and hunches over as girls huddle together, gossiping about the boys at the other end of the hall.

"Are you ok?" a girl with a jet-black pixie cut asks, approaching Aria.

Aria takes in her shiny nose ring and replies, "Mhmm."

"My name's Tessa. I've been here for a few months. I can help you find things or give you a tour, if you need it."

"I'm ok. Thanks."

"I've just seen that look in your eyes before," Tessa says in a low tone. "I know you need to be here. That you're scared. That you're running. I've got your back."

Aria sits back and drops her guard against Tessa. "Why are you here?"

"I've never had anywhere else accept me. Adrian and Eddy want me to stay until I find a good home." Tessa looks to the door, and her eyes turn glassy as if she's looking out an invisible window. "But this city chews up people like me. I'm never going to find somewhere to call my own."

"And you're ok here with all these people?"

Tessa sits on the bed beside her. "Not really. But this shows what's inside Adrian and Eddy's hearts. They won't turn anyone away. They don't want to be another one to turn their backs on someone in need."

"Do you think you'll ever leave?" Aria asks. "Do you have any family waiting for you?"

"There's no one I consider family anymore." Tessa's jaw grows rigid. "They treat me like a human being here. My so-called family treated me less than a dog."

Aria gulps and her eyes water at the loathing in Tessa's eyes. "I'm sorry. I didn't mean to upset you."

Tessa's expression eases. "You didn't. I've just been resentful the last few days. Some people here aren't running from anything. They're using this place as a playhouse. It's offensive."

Aria follows Tessa's gaze to the girls laughing on the other side of the room. "Do we have to listen to that all night?"

"They rarely spend all night here," Tessa explains. "It's getting close to midnight. They head off around this time to get wasted in the Nightclub District. Some stumble in at dawn, others you don't see again."

Aria's lip upturns and she shivers with repulsion.

"My head's pounding," Tessa says, standing. "I'm going for a walk. Wanna come?"

Aria stands. *What do I have to lose?* "Sure."

Aria takes one more look at the girls encircled at the other end of the room. Their dresses are short and tight, and they giggle between layers of makeup they add to each other's faces.

She follows Tessa down the hall and hugs her waist as they pass a group of young men. She feels their eyes on her and her skin crawls.

"You're not supposed to be up this end," Tessa says to them. "It's for women and children only."

"I'm a child," one guy replies. "Will you be my mummy?"

The group of males laugh together, and Tessa grabs onto Aria's arm and hurries her away from them.

"Sorry about that," Tessa grumbles as they move further up the hall.

"Not your fault," Aria murmurs, looking back at them.

A couple of guys looking at me in the hall are better than a jealous sister with a hammer.

"Like you said, they're going out soon."

"Right. We just gotta wait them out." Tessa sighs. "I'm going to be tired at work tomorrow."

"Do you work here?"

"No, I got a waitressing gig."

"Do you like it?"

"Not my dream job, but at least it's a job."

"I think I'd like a job."

"Have you met Jazz? She gave me some interview tips. You should see her before you go job-hunting."

"Yeah, maybe. Does she live here?"

Tessa snorts a laugh. "Heck no. She goes home at night to her ritzy mansion."

"Aria," a voice calls.

She spins around, grinning, as Eddy walks towards her. "Hi."

"It's late," he says. "I didn't think I'd see you up."

"We're waiting for our room to stop being a party zone," Tessa says sarcastically.

Eddy frowns. "Are you guys ok? Did anyone threaten you?"

"No, Tessa said they'd leave soon," Aria replies.

"We're fine," Tessa adds. "They're just loud. Believe it or not, it's quieter in the hall."

Eddy puffs a laugh. "That's hard to believe."

"Are you still working?" Aria asks, her eyes wandering along his shoulder, up his neck, across his lips, and landing on his eyes.

"I'm finished. I was hoping I wouldn't stay this late." He shrugs. "But that's the job."

"You like it?" Aria asks with hope.

Eddy smiles. "I love it."

Aria smiles, her shoulders easing with relief.

"Do you want to keep walking with me?" Tessa asks Aria.

Aria rubs her lips together, carefully pondering how to not come across as rude. "D'you mind if I talk to Eddy before he leaves?"

Tessa juts her mouth to speak, and her knees bend as she decides which way to move. "Ah... Yeah, uh... *Oh*. Yeah, ok. I'll see you later."

Eddy's cheeks turn peachy as laughter plays at his lips.

Aria looks down to the floor and lets her hair fall over her face, feeling as though her complexion is now redder than her hair.

"That was a little awkward," Eddy whispers.

Aria bites her lip and looks up at him.

"I'm sorry I haven't been able to spend any time with you."

"That's ok. I knew you would be busy when I was going to work with you."

"And you're ok staying here tonight?"

She nods, trying to look confident. "I think so."

"I'm heading home..."

I want to go with you.

"...I'd take you with me, but I don't think it's a good idea."

"Why?" It comes out before she can stop herself.

He hangs a thumb over his shoulder. "You wanna talk before I leave?"

Tingles energize her body. "Yes."

"I have one space in this place that's not overcrowded."

Eddy shows Aria down the hall and makes a path for her between the loud groups of people. He opens a door, and when Aria walks through the doorway, relief rushes through her body.

His eyes meet hers with a mix of happiness and concern. "How are you doing in here?"

"I like it here," Aria says as Eddy closes the door behind them. "It's crazy, but I like not being the centre of attention."

"It's the first time in a long time I don't know everyone's names out there," Eddy replies. "You can really get lost in the faces." He smiles and adds, "Not you though. I won't mistake that hair anytime soon."

Aria giggles, combing through her fiery hair. "It stands out a bit."

Eddy flops on the couch and slides his hands over his face. "What a day."

"You seem super stressed."

"I'm just tired."

"You never stop."

Eddy lowers his hands and connects with her eyes.

"Everyone needs someone to talk to." She remembers Adrian talking about Eddy to Gene. "You don't talk to your friends about how you're feeling?"

"I do, but my go-to is always to take on their problems. I can't stop myself."

"You need to take it easy or you'll explode."

Eddy lets out a weighted breath. "Honestly, all week I've felt like I could have exploded."

Aria slips her fingers between his. "Don't bottle up. You want to help me, and I want to help you just as much."

"Is it too overwhelming here?" Eddy asks, a distressed quirk to his lips.

"You're the one who seems overwhelmed."

Eddy bats his hands and tries to straighten his posture. "No, no, I'm ok."

"You should lessen your workload." She places a hand on his knee and watches his eyes drift to it. "You seem stressed to the max. You didn't seem like this at your apartment."

He finds her eyes. "I'm not hiding it, huh?"

She smiles and removes her hand. "Not very well."

"I'm trying to not seem agitated." He stretches his arms over his head. "I'm grateful. This place would have closed if not for Jazz. It's just so different to what we had in mind when we started out."

"How did you start this place?"

"It was a strange accident," he begins. "I was having another fight with my parents. About what I wanted to do with my life, and what they wanted for me. I took off through the Nightclub District and was heading towards The Limits. I don't know why. I guess it was because my parents would never step foot in that part of the city.

"Anyway, I came down to this area. My parents owned some warehouses down here. It was for development and an investment, but nothing happened with the buildings. I was walking through and found a bunch of kids squatting inside."

"Really? What did you do?"

"I had a knee-jerk reaction to call the cops," Eddy says. "But when I saw fear, hunger and loneliness on their faces, I stopped and talked to them. It was Adrian and a few other kids. They needed somewhere to stay. The city really had no place for them except for government group homes, which are not the safest.

"I convinced my parents to sign over the building to us. Adrian and I got on well straight away, and we had big hopes and dreams. We were making them happen, but money was an issue. We couldn't repair most of the building, but Jazz helped turn this place around. So, I know how well she means and how much we need her help, but she's gone too far in some areas."

"You need to help those who are already here. You can't help the whole city at once."

"Exactly." Eddy's green eyes brighten as he ensures he has her attention. "I wouldn't bring you here if I didn't think you'd be safe. We're being selective on who we give a bed to. It's just tough getting around to check on everyone." He frowns and looks away. "It's like I need two or three of me, at this point."

"You can't go on like this. You'll wear out," Aria says.

"Jazz wants to bring on another therapist."

"That would be good."

"Only if it doesn't mean keeping the current open-door policy. We need to ensure the truly vulnerable people can get in first."

Aria scrutinises his face as she takes in his words. "Sounds like Jazz both helps and hinders."

"She means more than well."

"You told me you loved what you do, but it seems far from it, right now."

Eddy exhales. "I'd never give myself permission to stop."

"Then I'll give you permission."

"That's the best thing anyone could have ever said to me," he whispers. "I'll work on lessening the load."

"I hope so."

"It's funny how someone else's permission makes things easier. What would be easier for you if someone else gave you permission?"

"Can I tell you a secret," she whispers.

"Of course."

"I've always wanted to perform on a stage. I've stepped on podiums to receive medals, but I'd love to be on a platform to sing a song. I'd give back every single trophy and medal for one moment like that."

"Would you sing for me?" Eddy asks, gazing into her eyes.

Goosebumps prick Aria's skin. Her heart patters in her chest, and she smiles nervously.

"Please?" he whispers with the sweetest smile. "You don't have to, but I'd like to hear you sing. And... I think you'd like to sing."

Aria's insides melt. In that moment, she's sure there's not a word he could say that would sound dangerous. She shakes out her arms, embracing the safety of his company.

"Ok," she whispers. A smile spreads across her lips.

She stands and clears her mind of everything except for hymns. She closes her eyes and a quiet hum seeps out of her in a melodic tune.

With her eyes closed tighter, her parents' voices creep into her head, telling her to shut her mouth. Her mother's tired and tearful eyes crowd her third eye.

She shakes out the image, opening her eyes. She stops the hum and finds Eddy staring at her intently.

"Sorry," she whispers.

"Don't be," he says, sitting forward. "You don't have to."

Aria stomps her foot, her hand curling into a fist. "But I want to."

Eddy smiles. "Then try. Don't let them in your head. It's just you and me here."

Aria holds her hands out toward him. "Will you stand with me?"

"Sure," he says, standing and taking her hands.

Aria holds them tight, closing her eyes again and letting out a steady breath. She takes in the room's emptiness and focuses on the texture of his hands. Strong, masculine, rough in places, smooth in others.

In the calm of Eddy's presence, her voice comes through. The tune, the pace, the breath. It all comes back. Like it was yesterday that she was in the choir. The sound pushes up from her diaphragm and ignites a light in her that was out for too long.

"Wow," Eddy whispers as she finishes her last line.

Aria laughs, happy tears lining her eyes. She squeezes his hands and says, "That felt really good."

"I don't understand why anyone would stop you from singing. You have a beautiful voice. You are allowed to be talented at more than one thing. And you, Aria, are."

Aria slips her hands out from his and wipes under her eyes. With a loud exhale, she flops on the couch. "They'll never let me."

Eddy sits beside her. "They can't control you."

"How did you tell your parents what you wanted to do?"

Eddy laughs, rubbing his forehead. "You don't wanna do it the way I did. There was a lot of yelling."

"I can't imagine you yelling."

"If I feel backed into a corner or near breaking point, I tend to raise my voice."

Aria pats his hands. "Hopefully that never happens to you again."

"That's why I keep my distance from them."

"And you're happy now?"

"Getting happier by the day," Eddy says, grinning as he slides his fingers by hers.

Aria bites her lip as a blush heats her cheeks.

"You need to be true to yourself," Eddy says. "You can't go back to your old life when that boot comes off your foot. You want to sing. You need to make it happen. Not singing is stealing your happiness."

"If I sing, I steal my parents' happiness."

"Your parents are proud of your accomplishments in the water. I'm sure they can shift to being proud of you out of the water."

"It's not that easy."

"I know it's not easy," Eddy says, slinging an arm around her.

For one moment, Aria wants to believe it's easy. That her parents will accept what she has to say and let her make her own decisions.

This room is small with a worn, black desk, a swivel chair, and a faded brown couch. It has an acrylic painting of the beach on one wall and tired, olive curtains covering the two small windows behind the desk. Despite its shabbiness, this room feels more like Eddy than the shallow, affluent apartment he spends his nights in.

She leans into Eddy and rests her head on his chest. Exhausted, she listens to the rhythm of his heart as he strokes her hair. For one moment, life is easy. She's happy. She's calm.

She closes her eyes.

Aria shivers herself awake. Blinking, she realises she's in Eddy's arms. He stirs awake, his arms loosening around her.

"You're cold?" he whispers in a sleepy voice.

"A little," she whispers back.

He sits up. "You want me to walk you to your bed?"

Aria pulls him by the shirt closer to her. "Nah-uh."

Eddy laughs in his sleepy voice and wraps his arms tight against her.

Aria likes the way his body is warm against hers. She likes being able to feel the gentle patter of his breath as his face slides close to hers. She likes everything about him. So much that she places her hands against the sides of his face and magnetically draws her lips to his.

Their kiss is soft and tender. Aria couldn't imagine a sweeter first kiss.

Her fingertips trace his jaw as their lips part. She smiles as he pulls his face back.

"I might be in love with you," he whispers, wrapping his arms around her.

Aria's mouth runs dry as she stares into his soulful eyes. She swallows hard and tries to still the tremor in her hands. "I think I might love you, too."

They lower on the couch, wrapped in each other's arms, and nestle their faces together. Their eyes close, and Aria wonders if this will be the first night in a long time she gets a restful night's sleep.

Safe

Eddy slides his arm out from under Aria's body. He smiles at the sweet look on her face as she sleeps. The morning sun streams in between the shoddy curtains and gives her lightly tanned skin a beautiful glow.

He tries his best to move without waking her, but when he slides down the couch, she stirs and blinks her eyes open.

"Good morning," he whispers, wearing a goofy grin.

Aria rubs her eyes and smiles back at him, sleepily. "Good morning."

"I was trying not to wake you."

"I can't believe I slept," she says in a groggy voice, stretching an arm above her head. "I never sleep."

"Who knew this couch could be so comfy?"

Aria reaches out and takes his hand. "You make me feel safe."

Eddy's heart thumps against his chest. His body warms, and he sits taller. He rubs a circle on her hand and smiles. "I'm glad. The last thing I want is for you to feel scared when you're here."

Aria sits up. "This place is not where I feel scared."

Eddy leans in and kisses her cheek. She rubs his arm as he does, and he's glad she feels comfortable with him.

He pulls back and says, "I don't want you to go home to a place that scares you. I want to protect you."

"I'll get in trouble if I don't go back."

Eddy looks to her moon boot and then back to her face. "I'm not letting anyone hurt you ever again."

Aria bites her lip and dips her gaze. When she looks up, she greets him with a smile that makes him melt inside.

"I believe you," she says.

"I really want to stay with you, but I need to get ready for work."

"I should probably leave. You'll have people coming in here to meet with you, right?"

"Yeah. Sorry. Want me to walk you back to the bedroom?"

Aria shakes her head. "No, I wouldn't get any more sleep. Are there showers here?"

"Yeah, I'll show you the way."

Eddy leads Aria into the hall, and notices Jazz coming from one end. He calls out to her, and she waves, moving their way.

"Do you mind if she shows you to them?" Eddy asks Aria.

"No, that's fine."

"Jazz, will you show Aria to the bathroom and where the towels and all that stuff is?" Eddy asks.

Jazz nods, smiling at Aria. "Sure, no problem."

"Thanks." Eddy turns to Aria and smiles, hiding some of his emotion while Jazz's eyes are on him. "I'll find you later."

Aria's grin mocks him with disbelief. "See you later."

"I'll try, at least," Eddy replies.

As the girls disappear up the hall, Eddy moves back to his office. Thoughts of Aria occupy his mind.

I want to make her feel special. Like she's the only person in the room. Like the only person who matters. I want her to truly know how wonderful she is.

He bounces in place. His mind develops a plan. Happiness

electrifies him.

Eddy's smile tingles his lips and grows bigger when he sees her.

"Aria," he calls out as he jogs towards her.

She stops and turns and greets him with her melt-worthy half smile. "Hey."

Eddy stops in front of her and laces his hands behind his back. Bashfulness battles inside him, and he tells himself to spit it out. "I was wondering if you'd like to go out somewhere with me tonight?"

A sparkle livens up her eyes. "Out somewhere?"

"I have somewhere in mind," he adds, shifting his weight. "A bar."

She chews her lip, apprehension dulling her features. "Oh, I dunno."

"I'm not talking about going to drink alcohol. It's a bar that has an open mic night," Eddy says. "I called them and they have a time slot open for tonight. They said you can take it. Would you be interested?"

Her mouth opens, ajar. Her eyes move from side to side, as she thinks on the proposition.

"What do you say?" Eddy asks, his enthusiasm weakening his nerves.

A grin lifts Aria's face, and Eddy's knees almost give way when her eyes meet his.

"I'd love to. That sounds amazing," she says. She steps in close and throws her arms around his neck. "Thank you so much."

Eddy rubs her back. "You're welcome. I'm glad you're excited about it."

Aria pulls out of the hug and stares at him with intensity. "It's nice to have someone who listens to me. No one's done that in a long time."

"I'll always listen to you. I care about you, Aria."

Her hand slides down his arm and grabs a hold of his. "Thank you. You're too good."

Revoked

Jazz shows Aria into the kitchen and asks, "Are you sure you want to be following me around today? Is your ankle hurting you?"

"The doctor said walking is fine," Aria replies. "Besides, I'll go stir-crazy on my own."

"Well, I don't mind showing you around. I know it helped me when I first came here to find ways to help."

"I can't believe you've only been here a month. I would have guessed you were the one who started this place."

Jazz smirks. "Because I'm such a control freak."

"I would have said because you seem so confident."

"That is a nicer way of putting it," Jazz replies. "Actually, my boyfriend started this place."

"Boyfriend?" Aria deadpans. "Do you mean Adrian?"

"Yes. You've met him?"

"Yeah." She drags out the word. "Sorry, I just didn't know you two were a couple. You seem so different."

"I know," Jazz says, eyes moving to a spot on the wall as she sighs. "I don't deserve him."

"He is a really nice guy," Aria replies. "And, hey, you're keeping this place afloat, so you must be a wonderful person too.”

“Thanks. I’m trying, but I have a long way to go on being patient.”

“You’re waiting for something?”

“I just want to make this place the best it can be.”

“I didn’t know this place existed,” Aria tells.

Jazz pushes her hair off her shoulder as she replies, “You must be the only person in Maiden City by now.”

“I never watch TV, but I heard there was an advertisement or something that brought people in.”

Jazz huffs. “The apparent open-door policy.”

“Sounds like it let in the wrong kind of people,” Aria says. “At least that’s what I’ve been told.”

“By who?” Jazz asks, eyebrow arching. “How many people?”

Aria shrugs. “A few.”

“Sorry,” Jazz says, backing away. “I shouldn’t be interrogating you. I already know I screwed up.”

“Gene said people manipulated what you said.”

“Gene’s just being nice,” Jazz says, displaying a limp smile. “He’s my cheerleader. Adrian’s right, I shouldn’t have done the interview. I was trying to impress my father and signal this girl I knew.”

“What signal?”

“There was a girl here when I first got here,” Jazz says, and sucks in a breath. “Her name was Myra. She vanished one morning, and I’ve never stopped wondering where she went. She told me about her past and her abusive partner. If I had asked her more questions, maybe I’d be able to find her. I hate the thought of her and her son back in an abusive situation.”

“You’re blaming yourself for her leaving?”

“No.” Jazz heaves a sigh. “Maybe.”

“Did she tell you she was leaving?”

"No. I was out for a run, and when I got back, they were gone."

"You can't blame yourself."

"I just want to know she is ok."

"There's nothing wrong with that."

"How long have you been wearing that brace?"

"For a week."

"So, you came here with Eddy?"

"Yes."

"Did you tell him what happened?"

"Um," Aria says, a squeak to her voice. "Do I have to answer that?"

Jazz steps back and frowns. "I'm sorry, I didn't mean to push. Have you known Eddy for long?"

"No," Aria says, shaking her head. "Just saw him at the pool a few times."

"He seems to really like you."

Aria giggles. "I really like him too. We have a kinda-date tonight."

Jazz's mouth hangs ajar. "Tell me more."

"He organised for me to sing at a bar tonight. It's so crazy. I've wanted to perform on a stage for so long. I can't believe he did this for me."

"That's so nice to hear," Jazz says, rubbing her hand over her heart.

"You know, we've met before."

"What do you mean? You and me? Like outside of the shelter?"

Aria grins. "Yes. At your gym."

"You're an Ultimate ME member?"

"No, I got a free pass when I won a swim meet. We met at a photoshoot, media thing." Aria plays with her hair and her freckled cheeks grow rosy. "Gene showed me a picture of us on your Collage feed."

"No way," Jazz says, pulling her phone from her pocket. She furiously scrolls, and then gasps as she lands on the picture. "My gosh, it is you." She looks up and meets Aria's eyes. "Please don't hold it against me that I didn't remember you."

Aria waves her hands, smiling. "Please don't worry about it. I didn't recognise you either. I pegged you as a supermodel until Gene told me about you."

Jazz laughs. "A supermodel? Hardly. But really, I'm sorry for not paying more attention to you back then. I was just far too work focused, attempting to make my way up the corporate ladder. It was the only way I knew to get my father's attention. And now that I don't work there, I'm struggling to communicate with him."

Aria sighs. "So, it's not easier once you leave your father's control?"

Jazz tilts her head, recognising the expression on Aria's face from her own mirrored reflection. "Are you asking for me or yourself?"

"I need time away from my family," Aria blurts. "I've done nothing but work to impress my father, too. He made me drop out of school early so training would be my only focus."

"Training for what?"

"Competitive swimming. I don't think I even like it anymore, but I want to keep him happy." Aria huffs, swinging her encased foot. "Now I'm out of the water for twelve weeks thanks to this stupid thing."

"He had nothing to do with it, did he?"

"No. He'd throw me back in the water with this boot on, if he could. It's killing him I'm out of the water."

"Sorry, had to ask."

"My father's obsessive, but he's not dangerous."

"Same with mine," Jazz replies. "My relationship with my father is still unsettled. I spent my whole life trying to impress him, and he still keeps Ethan under his wing after everything. Sometimes I think I should have been born a male. It seems the way to get instant respect in the business world, no matter how little you deserve it."

"Who's Ethan? Your brother?"

"No. My father mentors him." Jazz groans, imagining the pair in her father's office, making plans to dominate the industry. "Ethan made advances towards me, and my father still picked him over me."

"Advances?" Aria's voice squeaks and she jolts backward.

"He's a piece of work," Jazz says. "He even concocted a fake engagement."

"What?"

Jazz lifts a hand and raises her chin as she smiles. "But I'll put things right. One way or another. I'm still monitoring things over there."

"Doesn't it stress you out?" Aria asks. "To be working here and also trying to be present over there?"

"It stresses me out that I can't be present there." Jazz swallows roughly and her jaw tightens. "But it's good we can help so many people here. That looks good. Doesn't it?"

"I guess."

"There are kids from Province here. They are acting like this place is a party house."

"Can't you kick them out?"

"It feels like discrimination." Jazz sighs, head slumping in her hands. "No one kicked me out, even though I'm from Sovereign Hill."

"You feel bad because people helped you, and you want to pay it forward?"

Jazz raises her head from her hands and smiles at Aria. "You read me like a book. It's as if I don't know how to help. All my business training doesn't help me face to face with people. I don't have that skill."

"Like talking?" Aria asks. "I like talking with you."

"You remind me of Myra."

"The missing girl?"

"Yeah. Something about you makes me want to open up."

"Really?" Aria brightens. "I never had a real friend before."

"Truly?"

"Pa didn't encourage me to make friends."

"I was too busy trying to impress my father to keep any friendships myself."

"I have my sister, but I don't think we are friends."

"I would love a sister."

Aria's expression tightens.

"You look worried," Jazz whispers.

Aria breaks out of her thoughts. "Sorry," she replies.

"Don't be."

"Was your father ok with you working here?"

"It's hard to say. He gave me his blessing to leave the company."

"I don't think my father would ever give me his blessing to leave swimming."

"If you really hate it, you need to stop doing it." Jazz clasps her hand over Aria's. "We can help you. Did you chat to Eddy about tackling the topic with your father? He really helped me grow in confidence."

"Eddy seems to love what he does," Aria says. "I would love to feel like that."

"Working here gave me a sense of fulfilment I never knew I needed."

"That could be exactly what I need. Tessa said you helped her get a job and that you're easy to talk to," Aria says. "You don't feel good about that? It sounds like a success story to me."

Jazz purses her lips as she thinks on Tessa. Her father, Ethan and Myra fill her head and any thought of Tessa quickly minimises.

"Can you show me what you do here?" Aria asks and brings Jazz out of her thoughts.

"Sure. Ready to go back into the noise?"

Aria smiles. "Yes, let's do it."

Jazz leads Aria into the dining room, and they venture into the hall. The noise of a group of young males grabs her attention. She zeroes in on one individual in particular.

Jazz's blood boils. "Caden Walsh!" she yells, storming towards him. "What are you doing here?"

Caden tries *wooing* her with his trademark, charisma-oozing smile. "Miss Abadi, hello. I came to party." He turns to the guys behind him. "Ain't that right, lads."

Jazz pops a hip and slams her hand on it. "Nah-uh. You boys don't need refuge."

"You said all welcome," Caden replies condescendingly. "That even those with money can become invisible."

"You can already do that," Jazz fights back. "You're the Mayor's son. There's nothing you can't get away with."

"Abadi, lighten up," Caden smirks, sliding an arm around her shoulders.

His player moves give her the creeps. Especially in this place. A place meant to be safe from acts like this.

Jazz grabs his wrist and twists it until he yelps in pain. She swiftly turns his arm and locks it behind his back. He groans as she slams him against the brick wall.

"You think you got an open invitation to this place?" Jazz whispers harshly in his ear. "Well, consider that invitation revoked."

She lets him go and backs away. Her eyes move to Caden's friends and back to him. She points to the door and says, "Out. Now. Take your lads with you."

"You always were a buzzkill," Caden grizzles, straightening his designer shirt and loose tie.

"Make sure you don't come back," Jazz says with a fake smile and a quick wave.

"Wow," Aria says. Her mouth hangs open after she finishes the word.

Jazz rubs her forehead. "Sorry you had to see that."

"That was incredible," Aria says, stars in her eyes. "I've never seen a woman with such power. You should teach people here how to do that."

Jazz taps a finger to her lips. "Like a self-defence class?" She shrugs. "I could do that. I used to teach those classes as a personal trainer."

Aria's hands sit over her heart. "I would love to learn how to do that."

Jazz grins. "I'd be happy to teach you."

Peace

Valeria enjoys watching her mother struggle against the ropes. Her laugh is raspy as she tightens the knot by her mother's wrists.

"Valeria!" her father's voice shouts from the hall. "What on Earth are you doing?"

Valeria smirks. "Don't worry, Pappa. I'll get to you."

"Stop this immediately," he orders, marching towards them.

Valeria ignores her father, examining the bounds she made around her mother, who squirms on the dining chair.

"Why are you doing this to us?" her mother wails. "Are we such bad parents?"

Valeria's face screws up. *Duh.* I'm here to teach you how to parent. How to focus on me."

"Selfish," Angelo barks, grabbing Valeria's shoulder and spinning her around. "All you do is think of yourself."

Valeria tosses her father's hand off her. "You're the best at that. I must have picked up a few tricks."

"I do everything for this family," Angelo argues.

"As am I," she whispers viciously. "I'm making things right. I'm reshaping this family. I'll reprogram both of you to deal with it."

"We need to find Aria," her mother cries.

Valeria's eyes roll. "Oh, shut up."

"Do not speak to your mother like that," Angelo growls.

Valeria grins menacingly. "You want Aria back? Oh, I'll find her. I'll find her and you can make your peace."

"Peace?" her father questions. "Have you completely lost your mind?"

"No, Pappa. I very much know what I'm doing."

Her mother's whimpers increase in volume. Valeria notices her staring at the *Aria shrine*.

"Stop pining for her!" Valeria screams and slaps her mother across the face.

Her mother's face slams to the right, spit and blood flying out of her mouth.

"VALERIA," her father's voice booms.

Valeria retrieves a wrench from her back pocket and points it at her father with a steady hand. She looks him dead in the eyes with no expression.

"Don't test me," she says flatly. "Accept I now run this house."

"You hurt Aria, didn't you?" His voice shakes. "You broke her ankle to take her place."

A knock at the front door cuts the tension. Valeria keeps a hold of the weapon, staring down her father.

The knock sounds again.

Valeria grinds her teeth and turns to the door.

"Don't try anything," she says to her father, knowing he won't be able to untie her mother in a hurry.

She moves to the front door and opens it to find Tony on the front doorstep.

"Hi Valeria," he says cheerily. "I know we had a rocky start, but I was hoping we could go out again."

Valeria guffaws. "You really are a fool."

Tony's face falls. "Huh?"

"Call the police!" Angelo pleads, running from the kitchen. "Valeria's gone mad."

On instinct, Tony pulls his mobile phone from his trouser pocket. His face is a mess of confusion. "What?"

Valeria scowls and twists the wrench in her hand and bonks Tony over the head. He collapses to the ground.

"What have you done?" Angelo cries as Valeria drags Tony into the living room.

"You could give me a hand," Valeria grunts over Tony's unconscious body.

"Why are you doing all of this? Is this really because Aria is a better swimmer than you?"

Valeria dumps Tony's body by the sofa and wipes her brow with the back of her wrench-holding hand.

She stands tall and meets her father's eyes. "She's better than me because you pay attention to her. Maybe if you actually watched me when I swam, I'd be better."

"I don't watch you because you've already proven yourself to be a waste of time!" Angelo yells, spit flying out of his mouth.

Valeria's blood boils. Anger inflames her and all she sees is red as she ploughs the wrench into her father's stomach.

Angelo doubles over, wheezing and gasping for air. He stumbles backwards, tripping over his footing. As he falls to the ground, his head connects with the coffee table with an almighty crack.

Valeria sucks in a tight breath. "*Pappa*," she yelps.

She races to Angelo and strokes his thinning hair. "I'm sorry, I didn't mean to hit you."

He's out cold.

Valeria dips her face by his and witnesses him breathing.

She gets up and moves away from him. "You'll live."

She looks to Tony, whose chest rises and falls with uneasy breaths, and picks up his phone that lay by the door. She clicks some buttons and finds a webpage open to the bar he took her on their date.

Ick.

The page refreshes, and a set list appears.

Valeria glances at it and her lips curl. "Oh, you stupid girl."

Presence

Aria stands in front of the floor-length mirror as Gene shuffles through a rack of dresses. He dragged her away from Jazz as soon as he heard about the performance Eddy had lined up for her.

"What kind of dress do you want?" he asks.

"I dunno. Something pretty?"

Gene sniggers to himself. "That's a given. What kind of place is it?"

"I just know, it's a bar."

"I wonder if Eddy's around." Gene opens the door and sticks his head out into the hallway. He clicks his fingers and calls out, "Aid. Adrian, come here."

Adrian moves through the doorway, and Gene closes the door behind them.

"D'you know the place Aria's singing at?" Gene asks.

Adrian blows out a breath, looking up as he thinks. "Nah, I don't think so."

Gene shows him his phone screen. "Any of these look familiar?"

"Hmm, maybe this one," Adrian says, pointing to the screen. "The name sounds familiar." He looks to Aria and smiles. "Eddy talked through his grand idea with me to pump himself up to ask you."

Aria smiles, giddy. "I'm glad he did. I love the idea."

"I wish I were going," Gene grumbles.

Adrian laughs and tussles Gene's brunette curls. "You've got three years of growing up to do, and then you can go."

Gene groans and pulls away from Adrian.

"Are you excited for tonight?" Adrian asks Aria.

She nods. "And nervous."

"You'll do great," Adrian says, moving back to the door. "I'll catch you guys later, ok."

"Ok, bye," Gene says, scrolling on his phone. He slides next to Aria and shows her some photos of the lively bar. "This is the place. Looks like you can get as fancy as you like. Wanna look like a popstar?"

Aria giggles. "A popstar? Me? I don't think so. I'm used to singing church hymns."

Gene's lip upturns. "*Eww*, really?"

"Yes. Why does that make you say *eww*?"

"I dunno. Churches never seemed super welcoming to me. But I'm Jewish, so you can guess how much I care about your Catholic church," Gene says mockingly. "The only synagogue I wanted to go to was the one in Sovereign Hill, in hopes of meeting Jazz Abadi."

"That doesn't sound super religious."

"Well, I worship Jazz like a goddess, does that count?"

Aria laughs and nods. "Ok, I'll give you that."

Gene looks back at the rack of clothes with a heavy sigh. "I wish we were in Jazz's closet. We'd find the perfect dress in there." He leans on the rack, looking upward as he thinks. "She might let us... Oh wait, her dad lives there. She wouldn't want us mixing with him."

"He's way strict?"

"He'd probably think we were servants and accuse us of stealing or make us clean something."

"Have you met him?"

"Barely. I've been in the same room as him but haven't spoken to him. I'm just straight up assuming."

"My dad is way strict. But that's why I *don't* have nice clothes." Aria thumbs through the rack. "Everything here seems really nice to me."

"I love low expectations when people come into this room."

Gene gasps and slaps a hand over his mouth.

"What?" Aria asks with alarm.

"I forgot!" he cheers. Gene slides behind a cupboard and pulls out a dress bag. "When Jazz left her job to work here full time, she donated a heap of clothes. I sorted them out and hid the best pieces." He unzips the bag. "There are two cocktail dresses in here."

"What were you saving them for?"

"This moment," he whispers, slipping the dresses out of the bag.

Gene holds a black, shimmery cocktail dress in one hand, and a blush pink, sheer cocktail dress in the other.

"Wow," Aria hushes, walking up to Gene. "They're magnificent."

Gene bounces in place, grinning. "Which do you want to wear?"

Aria clasps her hands together, pursuing her lips. "I can't. These are too nice. They look so expensive."

"You deserve it," Gene replies. "Besides, Jazz donated them. They're up for grabs."

Aria exhales strongly as her eyes run along each dress.

Gene waggles the hanger holding the blush pink dress. "This one would really suit your complexion and highlight your hair colour."

Aria considers the dress. She shakes her head, noting how close the colour is to the walls of Eddy's apartment. The colour that his mother picked for her broken marriage apartment. She knows Eddy wouldn't like the reminder.

Aria holds out a hand towards the black dress. "I'll try the other one."

Gene hands over the dress. "Still a good choice. One sexy choice, I might add."

"Sexy?" Aria giggles. The word sounds foreign to her.

"Go try it on."

Aria moves behind the screen. "Ok, here goes nothing."

She slips out of the green, daisy patterned dress and unzips the side of the black dress. She steps into it and pulls it up her body. She frowns at her moon boot, hoping it doesn't steal focus while she's on stage.

Her reflection is odd. The most expensive item of clothing she's ever worn hugs her body. A chunky brace wraps around her foot, and the spaghetti strap shows off her ugly bruised shoulder.

The fact she's abandoned her family crashes over her. She hasn't let them know where she is, and they must be worried sick.

This is so wrong.

I can't leave my family like this. They gave up everything to make me an elite athlete, and now I'm going to walk away from it? How can I do this to them?

Aria takes some deep breaths and shuts her eyes tight. *Maybe I can do singing lessons while my leg heals. Then once I'm healed, I can swim and sing at the same time?*

If I can prove to my parents, I'm as good at singing as I am at swimming, surely, they'll let me do both. Then everyone can be happy.

Her stomach churns as she thinks of her parents' probable reaction to Eddy.

They'll be so disappointed in me.

They'll call me sinful for staying in his house. They haven't met him. I don't know if he's of our faith. And then we slept on the same couch?

They are going to be so mad at me.

Aria drops to the floor, her chest heaving. Her breathing becomes more laboured and she gasps in her next intake.

"Aria?" Gene's voice calls out with concern. "Are you all right?"

She wants to say yes. She doesn't want him to worry about her, but her fear devours her. She hunches over. Wheezing and panting. Her chest constricts and her throat closes in.

"Oh no, Aria." Gene frantically gets to her, rubbing her back and fidgeting beside her. "What's wrong? What can I do?"

Aria can no longer think.

She can no longer react.

She can barely hang on.

"*Shit*," Gene hushes. "I'll be right back. I'll be right back."

Gene whizzes out of the room, and Aria digs her nails into the vinyl flooring. Her sister's maniacal laughter thunders in her head. The hammer smashing her ankle replays over and over in her mind.

Footsteps hurry into the room and then someone plonks down beside her.

"Aria," Eddy's voice sounds strong and firm. "Aria, concentrate on my voice. Think about filling your lungs. Nice and slow." He takes her shoulders and gently pulls her up. "One nice long breath in."

Aria doesn't sit all the way up. Tears fill her eyes. Her face is red hot, and her hair clings to the sides of her face with sticky sweat. She whimpers in a pathetic breath.

"That's good. Keep trying," Eddy says in a soothing voice.

Aria closes her eyes and notices her heart slowing as she focuses on his voice.

She tries another inhale.

It's just as short.

"I'm going to count, ok, and you try to keep breathing in as I count."

As soon as he gets to two, frustration consumes Aria. He counts slowly and she can't hold on.

"It's ok," he whispers, rubbing her back. "Don't get mad at yourself. You can do it. Think about what you did last night to sing.

You held my hands, closed your eyes, and took a long breathe out. Try to envision that kind of calm. You can do it."

Aria slows her pace, remembering the magic of last night. How his presence is perfection. She sits higher, and her inhale lasts with his count of five.

"Good," Eddy cheers. "Now a slow exhale for five."

Aria manages an unsteady breath out for five beats.

Eddy rubs her back again. "Good work. Try to do it again until you feel steadier."

Aria keeps her eyes closed as she continues focusing on her breathing and listening to Eddy count.

"*Whoah*," Gene's voice sounds from behind them.

"Genie," Eddy says, "Mind giving us a minute?"

"Uh, yeah, sure, sorry," Gene says quickly, his footsteps leaving the room.

Aria opens her eyes, pats them dry, but can't bring herself to look at Eddy. Shame keeps her timid.

"What happened?" he whispers.

Aria's frown grows rigid to stop herself from crying.

"It's ok. You can tell me."

Aria shakes her head, staring at the floor.

"Is it about tonight?"

Aria clenches her insides

"Is it about home?"

A whimper tumbles out of her.

"You don't have to do this if you don't want to."

"I want to, but I don't think I can."

"You can do anything you want."

"I've never been allowed to before."

Eddy squeezes her hand. "You've never had me before."

Aria meets his eyes, and a fragile smile twitches at her lips.

"If you don't want to sing tonight, that's ok. But you decide. You control your life."

Aria squeezes his hand back. "Help me up?"

He smiles. "Sure."

Slowly, they make it to standing. Aria keeps a hold of his shoulders once she's upright, not wanting to let him go.

"Want to talk it out?" he whispers.

Aria shakes her head and moves closer to him, resting against his chest. Her smile warms as he rubs her back.

"Are you wearing this dress for tonight?"

"Yes. What do you think?"

"It looks great."

Eddy's hand carefully runs over her bare shoulder.

Aria winces. It's the first time he's seeing the bruises caused by her sister.

She switches injuries to avoid discussing it. "Even with the moon boot?"

"Anything looks good with you wearing it."

Aria buries her face in his shirt, a giggle bubbling inside her.

"Is it ok if I come back in?" Gene asks, slinking around the ajar door.

Aria steps away from Eddy and wipes her face. "Of course."

"Nice pick with the dress, Gene," Eddy says.

"It looks fabulous, Aria," Gene says, moving into the room.

She blushes. "Thanks."

"So, what do you think you will sing tonight?" Eddy asks.

"Heard this one?" Gene asks, hitting play on a song with his phone. "I love this chick."

A pop song plays through the speaker of his phone. Aria tilts her head as she listens to it. It's so different to anything she knows. It's scary and thrilling.

"Could I sing that?" she asks, an excited smile tugging at her lips.

"You'd rock it," Gene replies.

"Would you have time to learn it?" Eddy asks.

"It never used to take me long to learn a song," Aria says with a shrug. "If I listen to it enough times in a row, maybe."

"I'll keep it on repeat while I do your hair and makeup," Gene suggests.

"I'll let you get ready," Eddy says, patting Aria's hand. "I have someone to get back to."

"Sorry for pulling you away," Aria says, embarrassed.

"Don't be."

Support

Adrian summons all his courage and moves towards Jazz. "Can I talk to you?"

Jazz moves to the side with him. "Sure."

"I don't want to fight with you."

Jazz sighs and rests her hands on his shoulders. "I don't want to fight with you either."

"Will you join me at Aria's performance tonight?" Adrian asks, sliding his arms around her waist.

"Tonight?" Surprise fills her voice. "Can we leave this place at night?"

"I asked Hector and Maria if they'd mind staying back," Adrian says, edging his face closer to hers and taking in the sweet, floral notes of her perfume. "They're fine with it. We need to reconnect. We're drifting apart."

Jazz slides her hands down his chest and rests her forehead against his. "I know. Ok, I'd love to. Thank you."

"Really?"

A faint laugh escapes her. "Yes. Take me on a date, Mr Cassidy."

"My pleasure," he says with an almighty grin.

"So, what's the dress code?" Jazz asks.

"Yikes. I forgot about the dressing up part."

Jazz laughs. "True Adrian Cassidy, right there. C'mon, let's go see Gene."

They walk to the clothing room and knock upon entering. They find Aria standing in front of a mirror.

"Aria, you look gorgeous," Jazz says, her skin glowing with joy.

Aria blushes, pulling at the fabric of the dress. "You like it? You should, it's your dress."

Jazz smiles, shaking her head. "Looks like it's yours now."

"Thank you," Aria replies.

Adrian clasps Jazz's hand. "See how many people benefit from your generosity."

"I've been to thrift stores," Aria says. "There's never anything this fancy."

"Don't mention it," Jazz says. "It was nothing to give up some of my wardrobe. I'm not doing anything as helpful as Adrian does."

"Jazz," Adrian whispers, his heart sinking. "Don't keep putting yourself down." He kisses her hand. "You've helped so many people. You're amazing."

"Yeah," Aria agrees. "Like putting that dingus in his place."

Adrian smiles curiously. "Dingus?"

Jazz grins. "I kicked out a few of the preppy boys."

Adrian laughs. "*Whoah*. Nice job." He minimises his smile. "They didn't need help?"

Jazz shakes her head. "The Mayor's son doesn't need our help."

"What?" Adrian asks. "What was he doing here?"

Jazz sighs. "Taking advantage."

"Can I help?" Aria blurts.

"Huh?" Adrian and Jazz respond.

"Here," Aria says, grinning. "You two do so much to help the community. And Eddy loves what he does, even though he's overwhelmed. And..." She pauses to take a breath. "And I'd love to help. Can I stay and help?"

Adrian squeezes Jazz's hand, and they exchange knowing looks. Adrian turns to Aria and nods. "Of course. What would you like to do? Help people settle in? Help with preparing food? Help with cleaning?"

Aria smiles, clasping her hands. "Anything." She looks to Jazz with stars in her eyes. "I want to be brave like you."

"It's just ego," Jazz replies. "You don't want to be like me."

"Sure, I do."

"Well, if anything, I can give you those self-defence pointers we talked about," Jazz says, smiling.

"Tomorrow morning we'll sit down and talk, Aria," Adrian offers. "Tonight, it's all about you. Let's get you ready to perform."

"Where's Gene?" Jazz asks Aria.

"He went to the kitchen."

"No matter," Jazz says, thumbing through the racks. She winks at Adrian. "I can get us ready."

Aria bounces on the spot. "You guys are coming?"

"Hope that's ok," Adrian says.

"That's so cool," Aria hushes. "Thank you for the support."

Adrian smiles. "We're more than happy to come. I heard you have an amazing singing voice."

Fool

Aria's nerves buzz under her skin. She enters the bar with Eddy, Jazz and Adrian, and takes in the glitzy atmosphere. Cubes of blue light hang from the rafters, booth seating crowds small round tables, and elegantly dressed patrons hold uniquely coloured cocktails.

I can't believe I'm doing this.

She gathers her hair off her neck, the sweat creating an overwhelming body heat that pumps her heart too fast.

"If you're too nervous," Eddy says beside her, "you don't have to do it."

Aria clasps his hand and a smile fights against her apprehension. "No. I want to."

He smiles back, squeezing her hand. "Good, because I can't wait to hear you sing again."

Aria giggles. "Thanks for arranging this. And for asking me to sing again."

"You're welcome. I bet this place has better acoustics than those change rooms at the swimming pool."

Aria blushes. "I hope I don't make a fool of myself."

Eddy strokes the side of her face. "You could never."

"Ladies and Gents," the MC says into the microphone on the stage. "We have a newcomer tonight. Please welcome her to the stage. Give it up for Aria!"

Aria's heart hammers as the bar erupts in applause. *They haven't even heard me yet. What if they don't like me? Will they boo me off the stage?*

"Aria?" Eddy says beside her. "You ready?"

She smiles and finds comfort in the sincerity in his eyes. She nods and says, "Yes. Wish me luck."

"Good luck," Eddy replies, and Jazz and Adrian chime in with their best wishes.

With giggles, Aria sets off towards the stage. As she takes the steps up, the MC gestures to the microphone and then walks down the steps. Alone on the stage, she shivers with giddiness. She clasps her hands in front and takes a deep breath behind the microphone.

The music starts up.

No backing out now.

She closes her eyes and listens for her cue. The first two lines glide off her tongue. She keeps her eyes closed until a wolf-whistle grabs her attention. Her eyes open to adoring faces. Excitement chills her limbs. She drops her hands and puts more gusto into her words and powers through the melody.

As she changes tempo for the bridge, a person getting up from a table steals her attention. She muddles up a line when the person becomes Valeria.

She closes her eyes, begging her mind to stop playing tricks on her.

She opens her eyes and watches Valeria make her way up the aisle and towards the stage.

It can't be.

It can't be her.

Why would she be here?

Aria stumbles on the lyrics and then steps away from the microphone. There are collective grunts of disappointment from the audience.

Valeria races on stage and embraces Aria. "We've been worried about you," she whispers.

Aria tenses in her sister's grip.

Valeria pushes Aria toward the microphone. "Sing," she says in a soft, sweet voice. "Sing for everyone."

Aria swallows like she's being held by the neck. She eyes her sister and then looks back to the crowd. She notices Eddy shift in his seat and rise to standing.

I can't have Valeria anywhere near him.

Aria clears her throat away from the microphone, reorganising her energy to power through the last round of the chorus.

Valeria claps by Aria's side as the audience applauds. She slides over to microphone and cheers, "This is my sister, everyone. I hope you enjoyed hearing her beautiful voice."

The crowd claps louder and wolf-whistles echo through the room.

Valeria clasps Aria's hand and nudges her off the stage. "C'mon. We gotta get home."

Aria pulls back, her gut begging with her not to trust Valeria for a second.

"C'mon, Pappa's waiting." Valeria's eyes plead with her as they water up. "He's so mad. Please, come home with me."

Aria lets her guard down. "He's mad?"

Of course he is. I knew he would be. He's taking my disappearance out on everyone else.

"Is Ma ok?"

"She will be," Valeria replies. "If you come home with me now."

Aria nods. "Ok."

The sisters hold hands as they make their way off the stage and the MC introduces the next act.

Eddy makes his way over to them. "Aria, you were incredible." He moves in to hug her, but stops when his eyes focus on how close the sisters are standing. "Everything ok?"

Aria flashes him a smile. "Everything's fine. I'm going home with my sister."

"You don't have to go," Eddy says, his voice trailing off as he looks between the sisters. He looks down to Aria's moon boot and then back up to her face. "Will it be safe for you to go?"

"It's ok," Aria says, trying for confidence. "I want to go. My place is under my parents' roof. I need to go back."

"C'mon, Aria," Valeria says, a harsh edge to her words. "We can't keep them waiting."

Valeria drags Aria forward, and she stumbles as she tries to wave to Eddy.

"Bye," she whispers.

Eddy stares at her, dumbfounded. "No. Don't go."

Aria looks away, finding it too painful to take in his hurt and confused expression.

Jazz and Adrian stand in their path towards the exit.

"I'm ok," she says to them. "I'm going home."

"Are you sure?" Jazz asks, a wariness written on her face.

"I'm sure."

"We still have room for you, no matter how crowded," Adrian tries.

"We have to go," Valeria snaps at them.

"I need to go," Aria whispers, and she and Valeria keep moving towards the exit.

Outside the bar, Aria wriggles from Valeria's grip.

Valeria grabs her wrist tighter. "You're not getting away from me."

"Why are you trying to hurt me?"

"Because you deserve it!"

Aria's stomach churns, and her skin grows pale. "What's happening at home?"

"Get in the car," Valeria orders.

"Where's Pappa? What have you done with him?"

Valeria pushes her towards a car Aria doesn't recognise. "Get in!"

"Where are we going? Whose car is this?"

"Just shut up, Aria! You don't get to call the shots. Just get in."

Aria is moments off vomiting. She slides into the back of the car.

Valeria takes the driver's seat, and says, "We're going home to end this."

"End what?" Aria asks, shaken to her core.

Jealous

Eddy frantically races outside. "We need to find her! She's not safe!"

"Ed, Ed," Adrian calls after him. Adrian catches him and stops his panicked pacing. "Take a breath. Did she say where she lives?"

"Hamlet. But I don't know where."

Adrian looks to Jazz. "Did she tell you?"

Jazz shakes her head, her colour fading with worry. "No. Maybe Gene knows?"

Adrian snaps his fingers, thinking out loud. "They're from the same neighbourhood. Anyone know his address?"

Eddy fidgets in place. "I'd have it written down from when those social workers came for him. But I don't know it."

Jazz pulls her phone from her clutch and starts dialling. "I'll call him."

Eddy wipes his brows and brushes his hair back. "I shouldn't have let her go."

"She was with her sister," Adrian replies. "She said she wanted to go."

"Not with her eyes." Eddy fights to keep the contents of his stomach down. "She was abused at home. I know it. How could I let her go?"

Adrian squeezes Eddy's shoulder. "We'll get her back."

Jazz groans. "It keeps ringing out."

"He won't answer," Eddy says. "It's a madhouse in there."

Jazz tosses her phone in her bag. "Let's go to my place."

"In Sovereign Hill?" Eddy asks sceptically. "Aria lives in Hamlet."

"For my laptop," Jazz elaborates. "I have tracking software. Long story."

Eddy looks from Jazz to Adrian, who chews his lip nervously.

"C'mon," Jazz says, clapping her hands. "There's no time to waste. Let's find her."

Eddy nods. "I'm in."

"Ok," Adrian says hesitantly. "If you think you can find her."

"I need to pick Eddy's brain," Jazz says, texting her driver to bring the car around. "Anything Aria might have told you could be important."

Eddy thinks over all his moments with Aria, even the ones at the pool before they spoke a word to each other. A flash of her sister appears in his mind.

Aria barely spoke about her. They share a bedroom, but they aren't close.

He remembers the one-on-one with Valeria. How quickly she ran from hot to cold. Her flirty nature and then her aggression at the mention of their father. *Protective.* Eddy shakes his head. The manic look in Valeria's eyes burns in his memory.

"It's the sister," he blurts.

Jazz and Adrian halt, staring at him.

"The way Aria spoke about her father," Eddy continues, "she'd admit he was intense, but never alluded to him hurting her. I think her sister is the one that broke her ankle."

Jazz gasps and her hand shoots over mouth. "Oh my. I remember this look on Aria's face when we talked about her sister. Do you think she could really be capable of that?"

"I can't discount her," Eddy replies.

"She did snap at us when she and Aria were leaving," Adrian agrees.

"I didn't pay attention to her demeanour at first, because I've seen her act that way at the swimming pool," Eddy explains. "The first time I heard Aria sing, I was trying to have a conversation with her, but Valeria got between us and yelled that their father was waiting. And tonight, she went from sweetly embracing Aria, to brashly pulling her away when we tried talking to her."

"We'll find them," Jazz says tenaciously.

Jazz's car pulls up in front of them and they slide in. Eddy sits against the soft, black leather, and his knee bounces as his adrenaline runs high.

He digs his thumbs into his chin and watches Jazz and Adrian across from him for a distraction. There's an uncomfortable awkwardness shifting between them. Eddy's leg stills as he watches the pair.

"So, your place," Adrian says slowly.

"Mmm, yeah," Jazz replies with a nervous laugh. "I guess you had to see it sometime."

"Oh crap," Eddy blurts.

The two shoot him a look, the awkwardness heightening.

"This is your first time going to Jazz's house?" Eddy says.

"Well," Adrian says, tilting his head and wincing. "Not technically."

The air in the car grows stale.

Jazz grizzles and shakes her shoulders. "Let's discuss this later, shall we? Let's concentrate on Aria."

"Agreed," Eddy and Adrian say together.

Pain

Aria screams as Valeria pulls her from the backseat by the hair.

"Stop being a baby," Valeria snaps, pushing Aria towards their house. "Inside. We have an important meeting."

Aria's foot burns with a sharp pain inside the moon boot. Her ankle twists as Valeria forces her into the house.

"My foot," she whimpers.

"Shut up," Valeria orders, and slams Aria into the living room.

Aria falls onto the floor, gasping between sobs of shock. Her hands pulse with pain as she pulls herself up. When she looks ahead, the air is smacked out of her lungs.

Tony Moretti lies on his stomach, his eyes closed, and his tongue protruding out of his mouth. His hands are bound behind his back.

Aria checks he's breathing, and gasps again when she notes the gash on top of his head and the dark blood sitting in his hair.

"Don't worry about him," Valeria grumbles, pulling Aria up by the arm and tossing the car keys by Tony.

She drags Aria's pain riddled body along the floor and dumps her in the kitchen.

Aria pulls herself up to sitting as her mouth falls open.

"Mamma?" she says in hushed panic.

Her mother sits in a chair. Her hands bound behind her back, and her legs tied to the chair legs. A large purple bruise to her left cheek.

"What's going on?" Aria asks, trembling, in the dimly lit room.

Valeria shooshes her, pacing around Aria and swinging a wrench by her side.

"You've been tying up our parents?"

Whack.

Aria cries in pain, clutching her arm. Under her hand, her flesh pulsates with red hot pain where Valeria swung the wrench. She tumbles forward. The pain shoots into her brain.

"You shut up, Aria!" Valeria yells, looming over her sister. "You don't get to talk. I run this house."

Aria shivers under Valeria's volume. *Dear God, what has she done while I've been gone?*

Valeria circles her mother and pats the top of her head. "I found her singing, Ma."

Through squinting eyes, Aria watches her mother whimper and thrash against the ropes.

"Her singing pains you so," Valeria taunts, nestling her face by her mothers. "She knows that, but she abandoned us and did it anyway. And did it dressed like a Jezebel. I even found her with a man."

"Aria," her mother yelps. "How could you? After everything we've sacrificed for you."

Aria sits up, her head aching, and watches her mother's sweat-stricken face redden. Aria's heart jackhammers as her mother's composure spirals into hysteria.

"Mamma, it's not like... I've sacrificed... I'm sorry..."

Crack.

Valeria swings the wrench into Aria's arm.

Aria collapses, face first, onto the floor.

Strong

Adrian fights his nerves as he walks into the foyer of the Abadi Mansion.

"I'll be right back," Jazz says, hurrying from the foyer into a lavish living room and up one side of the winding dual staircases.

"I can't believe she's gone," Eddy says, pacing by a chaise lounge.

A slick sweat runs down Adrian's neck as he looks at the most expensive lounge he's ever seen. He feels unworthy just looking at it.

Adrian turns his attention to his anxious friend and slides towards him, taking a hold of his arms. "Bud, you gotta chill. I know you're scared, but we'll find her."

"She's already got a broken ankle, and there are bruises to her shoulder," Eddy says, fear coating his words. "We let her go back into that house."

"We won't make that mistake again."

"Got it," Jazz says, taking the stairs down two at a time. "Eddy, what's her last name?"

Eddy rubs his temples, thinking. "They talked about her family at the pool kiosk." He huffs, trying to recall the name. He drops his hands and opens his eyes. "Rivera."

Jazz lands on a couch and types furiously on the keyboard. "She's a national champ, right?" More typing and Jazz grins. "There's my girl."

Eddy slides behind Jazz. "You found her?"

"I found articles on her winning the state championship. I'll dig from here."

"How did you get this software?" Eddy asks, peering over her shoulder at the screen.

"Never mind that."

"No. How did you get this?" Eddy says, firmly. "It seems super illegal."

Jazz recoils. "In the wrong hands, maybe."

"Jazz?"

She huffs. "Fine. I got it from Ethan."

"Ethan?" Adrian asks, his stomach dropping.

"Yes. He was trying to make things right. Make up for the past."

"By giving you access to people's locations and personal records?" Eddy says.

"Can't we just focus on finding Aria?" Jazz says defensively.

"Why do you have this? Why did he give this to you?" Adrian asks, disturbed. "You two have been talking? Meeting up?"

"My father sent him," Jazz says. "They want me back at the company. At the very least, heading up the social media department. I said no, and Ethan asked how he could help me."

It repulses Adrian. "You're taking help from Ethan Roth?"

"I told him I didn't want his help. I was talking about doing real work. Actually helping people," Jazz defends herself. "When I mentioned wanting to find Myra, Ethan said he had the means to track her down. I'd seen the surveillance he had on me. He didn't pinpoint my location, but I had a hunch Myra might leave a trail. So, I accepted his help."

"Ethan has been looking for Myra?" Adrian asks, disgust to his voice. "He's a predator."

"He just gave me the software and told me how to use it. He's not looking for her."

"I can't believe you're still talking to him."

"I'm not talking to him," Jazz says, exhausted. "He gave me this with the goal of swaying me. I never had the intention of reciprocating or going back to Ultimate ME."

"Why didn't you tell me about it?" Adrian asks, crossing his arms. Jazz looks down.

Adrian turns away, unable to take in her hurt and frustration. He didn't want to be angry at her, but how can he be in love with someone who would stoop to this level?

"I was ashamed," she whispers. "I felt guilty. I knew it was wrong, but I was desperate to impress my father. He doesn't take me seriously and is banking on me messing up my life."

Adrian unfolds his arms and turns back to her. "You need to stop measuring your self-worth by what he thinks. You chose to volunteer at the shelter. Own it."

"I do."

"Do you?"

"All right," Eddy interrupts. "I can't take this anymore. Jazz, what you've done is messed up, but I can't sit her while Aria is in danger. Can we find her and work all this out later?"

"I'm sorry," Jazz says.

"Me too, Ed. We'll find her," Adrian says. "I promise."

Eddy groans and pushes his hands into his stomach. "I'm gonna hurl."

Jazz turns and snaps her fingers at him. "You're useless to Aria if you fall apart. She needs you to be strong right now."

Eddy lets out a long breath for three beats and nods.

Jazz's fingers hurry over the keys of her laptop. "Here's an address in Hamlet. It's sourced from the Maiden City Swimming Pool client files. Shall we roll with it?"

"Let's get in the car," Eddy says, running to the front door.

Jazz slides the laptop off her lap and stands to follow Eddy.

"Hey," Adrian says, placing his hands up to get her to stop. "Can we talk for a minute?"

"We need to find Aria."

"I'm standing in your house," Adrian says, his knees seconds from knocking. "Does this not freak you out?"

"Adrian," she sighs. "Can we not do this right now?"

"You still don't forgive me."

She looks him in the eyes. "What?"

"For the locket."

She groans. "I don't care about the locket."

"You must. You keep pulling away from me, and you've been with Ethan."

"This isn't about Ethan," she argues, raising her voice.

"Was he the person on your secretive phone call?"

Guilt colours her face. "He told me he had a lead."

"You said he wasn't looking for her."

"He's not. He lied to get me on the phone," she explains, irritated. "That's why I didn't tell you. He was messing with me and not worth talking about."

"Anything in your life is worth discussing."

"We need to stop talking about him. This is about Aria."

"We've been distant since before meeting her."

"I won't have another mistake on my watch," Jazz says with a stamp of her foot. "I won't let one more girl go missing who should have stayed safe."

"She's not Myra."

Jazz beckons him to follow. "We need to get going."

"Adrian," Eddy calls from outside. "Jazz. Let's go."

Abandon

Aria's pain is too much to bear. She was too weak to fight off Valeria tying her up, and now sits on the floor, crouched with her wrists bound to her ankles.

"You are such a stupid girl, Aria," Valeria scorns, slamming the wrench between Aria's shoulder blades.

The pain reverberates down her spine. Tears spring from her eyes, and her vision triples.

"Valeria!" Angelo yells with a raspy voice. "Enough. Stop this madness."

Hope ignites every cell in Aria's body. She looks for her father in the darkened room.

In the hall, between the living room and the kitchen, his slumped and bound body sits on the floor. His head fights to stay upright, showing his groggy state. Aria guesses he had been out cold like Tony currently is.

"Madness?" Valeria questions, moving towards her father with the threatening weapon. "Madness is choosing her over me. All I've done is be loyal to you. Time and time again, you pick my little sister. I could have been the best, but you favoured this pathetic mess." She points the wrench at Aria for emphasis. "Why? Why is she the favourite?"

"She's better," Angelo answers, and spits at Valeria's feet.

"Pappa no!" Aria screams.

She's too late. Valeria swings the wrench. Aria scrunches her eyes closed, waiting for the crack.

Her eyes open when Valeria's let's go of an ear-piercing screech. The wrench is whisper close to Angelo's jaw, but doesn't connect.

"Valeria, stop this!" Aria yells, scratching her throat. "I'm who you want. Leave them alone."

Valeria turns, stomps over to her, and slaps her across the cheek.

"You don't run this house!" Valeria snaps. "I do. Stop trying to control me."

Aria spits out blood and anger pumps through her heart.

"Fine," Aria says, a new form of confidence surging through her veins. "You're in charge. I'll do what you want."

"Don't make me out as a fool," Valeria says, pacing.

"But you are in charge," Aria says with as much conviction as she can muster. "You always have been. I've always feared you. You're stronger than me. You remind me every night before bed. You are the best out of the two of us."

"My goodness," Valeria smirks and stops pacing. "You said one non-dumb thing. How rare for you, dear sister."

Aria gulps, looking from Valeria to her parents. Her father's chest rises and falls much too quickly against the ropes tied around him. His face red and perspiring. Her mother is a sobbing mess with fear slathered over her face.

"I, I..." Aria stumbles on her words, trying to appease Valeria and stall for her parents' sake.

Smack.

Valeria strikes Aria's face again, this time with so much power,

Aria's head hits the floor.

"You're not in charge, dear sister." Valeria whispers, leaning over Aria. "Now, stay down."

Valeria twirls the wrench, stepping over Aria, and walks towards the back door.

The door opens and closes again.

She's gone.

"This is all your fault," her mother says with a layer of revulsion to her words.

Aria lifts her head, squinting in pain. "Huh?"

"You left and drove Valeria insane," her mother blames. "We've been living in a state of Hell because of you."

"Ma, I'm sorry," Aria cries. "I didn't think she'd hurt you. I thought she'd be better with me gone."

"You can't stay away," Angelo says, slurring his words.

"I can't stay," Aria says, breathless. "I can't live like this. No one can."

"You ran away," Angelo accuses. "No one kidnapped you. You purposefully left us."

"It wasn't like that."

"Aria," her mother sobs. "How could you?"

"I'm not a little girl anymore," Aria argues, scrunching her eyes closed and digging deep for bravery. "You can't force me to keep living this life."

"What are you saying?" Angelo presses, fighting to keep his head up in his woozy state.

"I'm not going back to swimming."

"Don't be ridiculous." Angelo pulls himself upright, his power coming back. "Once that thing is off your foot, you are going back into the water."

"I found a job."

"What good will you be out in the world?" He groans in pain.

"You have no skills. No education."

"You did that on purpose, so I'd be stuck here. Is this really what you wanted? All of us held captive in our home?"

"Stupid girl. No one is going to hire you."

"I didn't ask for this," Aria fights back, tears rolling from her eyes.

"Ungrateful," Angelo hisses, his head slumping once again.

"I want to be more than a swimmer," Aria begs.

Her mother bawls in frenzied sobs. Her body shakes violently enough to topple the chair.

"*Mamma*." Aria's heart slingshots in her chest. "Ma, I'm sorry. I want to make it better. Please, I'll be better. Don't cry."

Dead

Eddy leaves the car and hurries towards the house they suspect is Aria's. Jazz and Adrian trail behind him.

"Jazz," Adrian whispers, holding out a hand toward her. "You ok?"

"I'm going to call the police," she whispers back.

Eddy stops and turns as Adrian says what he was thinking, "Police? Are you sure that's a good idea?"

"We'll get Aria to safety," Jazz replies. "But I don't want these people coming after her. They need to be behind bars."

"I'm going on ahead," Eddy whispers.

"I don't want to leave you on your own," Adrian says to Jazz.

"I'll be fine. You know I can hold my own. Really, go."

Adrian moves forward and signals to Eddy he'll move down the opposite side of the house.

Eddy stealthily makes his way along the side of the house. Panic fills his veins and terror looms over his thoughts.

Aria is dedicated to her family.

I've seen her give up before. Sacrifice herself.

He wipes the sweat from his brow.

I won't let that happen again.

Eddy pads the wall and tries to peer through the window. The curtains are drawn and no lights are on inside. With all his might, he tries to reef open the window, but it's bolted shut.

He moves further to the back of the house and muffled shouts and screams make their way outside.

His heart leaps in chest, and his feet dig into the earth. More than anything, he wants to call out for Aria, but he doesn't know what kind of situation she's in. The last thing he wants to do is make anything worse.

He views the backyard and spies a tool shed by the fence line. Aria had mentioned a tool shed around the same time she was talking about her sister's envy.

He shivers against a cold that comes from within.

Could those screams have come from down there?

He breathes deeply, in and out, and creeps through the backyard. The night casts shadows over everything, and he squints at the shed. The door opens and someone exits. They drag something out of the shed, and then return inside.

Eddy stops dead. His gut tells him to not go down there. He can't explain it, but he turns toward the house. He'll check if the house is empty, and then regroup with Adrian and Jazz, and collectively make their way to the tool shed.

Carefully and silently, he approaches the back door of the house. He gently turns the doorknob and slowly pulls the door open.

"You need to stop this!" Aria's voice screams.

"Aria?" it breathlessly races out of him.

"Eddy?" her voice trembles in fear. "What are you doing here? Get out of here! It's not safe!"

Eddy rushes into the house, terror and adrenaline coursing through his body. He scans the darkened room and spies a fallen chair, a body strapped to it, and then Aria's crouched body.

"*Aria*," he gasps, running to her.

His hands rush to the sides of her face, and she shakes her head, tears filling her eyes as she says, "Help my mamma."

Eddy spins to the fallen chair. Aria's mother convulses against the chair she is bound to. Eddy is quick to lift the chair to its correct position, using all his strength to keep Mrs Rivera upright.

As he looks at the ropes against her wrists and the masterful knots, Aria tells him between panicked breaths, "My dad is in the hall. He's hurt. And Tony is in the living room. His head is covered in blood."

Eddy moves to the hall and finds Aria's father fallen in a heap with ropes tied around his body.

Angelo stirs and pulls himself up. His eyes land on Eddy and enlarge with a jolt. "Who are you?"

"I'm here to help you," Eddy says, looking at the bruising to Angelo's head.

Angelo thrashes against the ropes. "Why are you here? Are you helping my daughter do this to us?"

"Try to remain calm," Eddy says, having trouble doing that himself. "We need to get out of here, and you need to keep your strength."

"Strength?" Angelo questions agitatedly. "I'll show you strength."

"*Pappa*," Aria calls. "He's here to help. Don't fight him."

"You!" Angelo's eyes centre on Eddy with repugnance. "You're the one who has been keeping Aria from us!"

"He hasn't been keeping me anywhere," Aria cries.

"Aria needed to get away from here," Eddy tells Angelo. He looks back to the dining room and adds, "Clearly she was right."

"How dare you!" Angelo yells, enraged. "I keep my girls safe. Not you!"

"Safe?" Eddy replies, anger stirring inside of him. "This is keeping them safe?"

"I will stop Valeria," Angelo retorts. "I will make her stop this, and I will take control of this family again."

"You have to know controlling their lives is doing your daughters harm."

"What do you know of it? Only I know what's best for them!"

Fury explodes in Eddy. The kind he hasn't felt in years. He eyes Angelo, and yells, "Then why did Aria choose to drown herself, instead of living under your roof?"

"Eddy, no!" Aria gasps.

Eddy turns to her, anguished by the tears rolling down her face.

"The pool," Angelo murmurs. "Keats told me... It was true?"

"Aria, I'm sorry," Eddy says, keeping his eyes fixed on her. "I didn't mean to—"

"—Watch out!" Angelo warns.

On instinct, Eddy ducks.

Whoosh.

He looks up as a large, heavy mallet soars in the air where his head was. He spins around and Valeria pulls the mallet towards her and sets it by her feet.

A depraved grin spreads her lips, and her eyes are unblinking.

"You weren't invited to the party," Valeria says with a smirk.

Eddy stands, and within half a second, Valeria charges at him.

He lunges out of the way.

A high-pitched scream gurgles out of her. She hoists the mallet and thrashes it toward him.

Eddy backs away, scrambling to keep his footing.

Valeria rampages at him, backing him to the door. She pushes him outside with the force of the mallet, and slams the door shut.

Eddy's heart jackhammers inside of him. He leaps towards the back door and pounds on it.

"Hey! Hey! Let me in! Aria! *Aria!*"

Life

Aria's breath burns in her throat as her heart smacks against her ribs.

"No!" she screams, cloaked in terror at the thought of Eddy getting hurt. Jazz and Adrian are probably outside too.

Valeria drops the mallet by Aria's cowering body. Flames of hatred in her eyes. "Told your boyfriend where we live?"

"Don't hurt them," Aria whimpers.

"Dear sister," Valeria says, her voice almost melodic. "You're the only one I want."

"Then fine," Aria blurts, sitting higher. "Take me. Take me and leave everyone else alone."

"Aria, no," their father calls. "Valeria, I've hurt you. Take me."

"Shut it, Pappa," Valeria snaps. "You and Ma aren't going anywhere."

Valeria pulls a knife from her back pocket and Aria's heart stops for a beat too long.

Aria gulps as her sister stomps toward her with the pointed knife.
Slice. Slice.

Two quick movements, and the ropes around Aria's wrists and

ankles are cut.

"Get up," Valeria orders, sliding the knife inside her belt and picking up the mallet. "We'll end this. Now."

Aria rises, taking a moment to look at her parents, preparing herself for never seeing them again. For seeing no one again.

As long as everyone else is safe, it'll be ok.

Valeria smashes the mallet into the back door, splintering the wood and sending pieces soaring out to the backyard.

Eddy yells in alarm.

Aria's heart pounds. She leans forward to see if he's ok.

Valeria grabs a tuft of Aria's hair and drags her through the doorway.

Aria cries out in pain and her limbs scrape against the ground from Valeria's speed and force.

"Aria," Eddy's voice breaks through, and she swivels her head to gain a view of him.

His reddened eyes droop with fear and sadness.

Her eyes plead with his. "Go," Aria says in a raspy voice.

Eddy moves forward, and Aria yearns to scream out *no*, but Valeria reefs her backwards.

Aria falls onto her back with a thud. Her sister looms over her in the moonlight, and it all feels frighteningly too familiar. As she watches Valeria lift the mallet high, a tear falls from her eye.

"You don't get to win," Aria whispers.

Valeria swings the hammer downward, and Aria rolls herself to the side as the mallet thunders into the ground.

An animalistic groan grumbles out of Valeria as she almost loses her balance, pulling the mallet up.

"Aria!" Eddy calls with panic.

"I'm ok," she calls, getting up. "Get out of here before you get hurt."

Valeria slams her body into Aria's, knocking her to the ground.

Aria coughs, writhing on the ground, her lungs deflating.

Valeria cackles to herself until she falls to the ground.

Wheezing, Aria searches beside her.

Eddy crawls into view, touching Aria's arms and face.

"Are you ok?" he asks with a mixture of relief and dread.

Aria scans their surroundings. "Where? Where?"

Eddy strokes her hair. "I knocked her down, but she's moved up to the side of the house. I'm not leaving you alone."

Overwhelmed, Aria struggles against him to get up. "No! No!"

The worst thing in her mind is letting Valeria on the run.

Eddy cups her face. "Breathe. Sweetie, breathe. We'll be ok. We'll be ok if we stick together."

Aria stops and doesn't let the panic drive her. She looks at Eddy properly for the first time. His eyes shine and fill her with life.

A tear falls from her eye, and she loops her arms around his neck. She trembles as she says, "Oh my gosh. I'm so glad you're here. I love you so much."

Eddy kisses her. "I love you too. I'm sorry for what I said to your father."

"Don't be sorry."

"I didn't mean to say it. I let my anger take control."

"Maybe anger is what we need," Aria says steadfastly. "To stop Valeria."

"I won't let anything bad happen to you. I promise."

"She wants to kill me."

"It's not going to happen."

"We need to stop my sister."

Afraid

Adrian heard the screams, but the overgrown foliage stopped him from racing to the backyard. His arms are scratched and his trousers torn from trying to get through the bushes.

He groans and pushes through the last bush. He sighs out in relief when he makes it through, but then something hits him from the right.

He falls backwards, and his torso pulsates from the attack.

Valeria charges at him, swinging her mallet from side to side, with madness in her eyes.

Adrian cowers and lifts his arms over his face in an X position.

When Adrian braces for the next attack, Jazz's voice rings out.

Jazz surges from the bushes behind him and knocks Valeria to the ground. "Stay away from him, you crazy bitch!" she yells.

Jazz fights Valeria for control of the mallet. Valeria growls and pushes Jazz off her. Adrian pulls himself up to grab Valeria, but she darts away with the mallet.

Adrian moves to follow, but Jazz pushes him back. She places a hand over his beating heart and smooths back his hair with the other.

Her eyes round and she swallows roughly. "I don't know what I'd do if anything happened to you."

He gently takes her wrist and whispers, "I'm ok."

"Out of everyone in my life," she continues, "you're the person I care most about. I don't know why I've been so afraid to show that."

Adrian's breathing falters as she moves in closer to him.

Her lips are an inch from his. "I love you, Adrian."

He blinks at her. "You do?"

Her lips push onto his. Her hands run into his hair, and for a moment they are away from the chaos.

She pulls away and whispers, "I really love you."

He dares a smile. "You're badass and I love you."

She grins. "Let's get this bitch."

Charge

Eddy holds Aria tightly. Tears sting his eyes as he runs his fingers over the fresh wounds to her arm.

An ominous thud breaks them out of the tender moment.

Eddy looks around the space and sees the mallet that hit ground by their feet.

"Miss me?" Valeria taunts.

Valeria yanks back part of Aria's hair and draws a knife from her belt.

"No!" Eddy shouts, holding onto Aria's waist.

Valeria kicks her boot into Eddy's chest, forcing him to let go of Aria.

"Stop this," Aria yelps, fighting against her sister.

Eddy scampers to standing as Valeria holds the knife against Aria's neck.

"Put the knife down," Eddy says calmly, his hands pushing out like stop signs, and he lowers his frame.

"This is between me and her," Valeria yells. Her face shines red and determination glows in her eyes. "Do you really want to stick around to see her end?"

"She's your sister," Eddy tries to reason, not taking another step closer. "You don't want to kill her."

"You don't know me," Valeria fires back and digs the knife into Aria's skin.

Aria yelps as fresh, crimson blood drips down her neck.

"Stop!" Eddy yells, panic knocking his knees.

"You're outnumbered," Jazz yells as she and Adrian race into the yard. "Put the knife down!"

Aria's eyes pivot between them all. Purpose shapes her face. Her chest heaves and then she slams her moon boot onto her sister's foot.

It was enough for Valeria to loosen her grip on the knife. She groans and shifts backwards.

Eddy, Adrian and Jazz charge towards the sisters. The boys pin Valeria to the ground. She thrashes against their weight, but they have her.

Thank God, Eddy thinks.

Jazz embraces Aria and applies pressure to the gash on her neck.

"I'm ok," Aria says with laboured breaths.

Sirens and flashes of blue and red lights fill the street.

"Where are your parents?" Jazz asks.

"Inside. She tied them up."

"Police!" a voice sounds through a megaphone. "We have the house surrounded."

Uniformed officers run into the yard. They pull Adrian and Eddy off Valeria and cuff her. Before Valeria can utter another word, the officers escort her to a police van.

A paramedic tends to Aria, and Jazz shows other officials into the house to tend to Mr and Mrs Rivera.

The blade had nicked Aria's skin. After they apply a bandage, Eddy is quick to scoop Aria into his arms.

He nuzzles his face against hers. His heart runs a mile a minute, and he wishes it would slow down so it doesn't upset her.

She holds onto him tighter, and even though she's shivering, her body is warm.

There's nothing he can say that can capture the happiness, relief, and love he feels in this moment. He soaks up her presence and never wants to let her go.

Lucky

Aria stands with Eddy helping her up. Her ankle pulsates in pain from slamming it against Valeria's foot, but it was worth it.

"You were so brave," Eddy whispers.

"I wasn't going to let her hurt anyone," Aria says.

The magnitude of what her sister tried to accomplish tonight fully hits her.

She's not well.

Eddy kisses the top of her head and helps her towards the front of the house. Ahead, Aria sees Tony Moretti being lifted on a gurney into the back of an ambulance.

"He's going to be ok," an officer says, walking by them. "It's a serious head wound, but they are optimistic."

"Thank you," Eddy says on their behalf.

"My parents," Aria says breathlessly as a paramedic checks her mother and father by the front of the house. "Are you two ok?"

"How could Valeria do this?" her mother says, shellshocked.

"It's ok," Aria coos. "She's gone now. We're safe."

"Safe to do what?" Angelo says. His tired face sagging into depression.

"We're going back to the shelter," Eddy says to Aria's parents. "We have room for you. Come with us and we can help you heal."

Angelo crosses his arms and lifts his chin. "We will go to the police station. To be there for Valeria."

"*Now* you'll be there for her?" It flies out of Aria's mouth before she can bite her tongue.

"We need to fix what we did," he replies and hangs his head in his hands. "I'm the reason she did this."

"Valeria needs help," Aria says. "Maybe we could all do with some therapy."

Angelo scoffs, lowering his hands. "And, what are you going to do, Aria?"

"I'm moving into the shelter," she says, clutching Eddy's hand. "I can't live with you two. Not for a while."

"You're really leaving us?" her mother whimpers.

"Mamma and Pappa," Aria says, "go back to church. Go back to the family. It will make things right. That's where happiness is."

Her parents shift and avert their eyes from her.

She's too exhausted to convince her parents of anything. Aria hopes time can heal their internal wounds, and if their visit with Valeria can help her mental state, she'd be grateful.

She squeezes Eddy's hand and signals for them to keep moving.

"Young man," Angelo calls.

They turn around, and Angelo adds, "Make sure no harm comes to Aria. I'm trusting you."

Aria's heart squeezes, and a smile dares to curl her lips.

"His name is Eddy," she tells her parents.

Her father nods. "Eddy."

Her mother's tear-soaked eyes shine, and she nods too. "Eddy."

Eddy kisses the top of Aria's head, and says, "I will. You can be sure of that."

Aria and Eddy move toward Jazz's car.

"Are you ok?" he asks, tentatively holding Aria upright.

"I will be. I just want to be away from here." She rests her head on his shoulder as they plod their way forward. "I'm finally rid of my sister. Now all I want is to be with you."

"You have me."

"How did I get to be so lucky?"

Love

Jazz wraps her arms around Adrian's waist, the pair alone in his office at the shelter.

"I'm sorry for not being honest with you," she says. "I should have told you about Ethan."

"After everything that happened tonight, I'm ready to forget Ethan exists."

"I should do the same thing."

"I wish you had told me," Adrian says, running his hands down her back. "But I understand why you did it."

"It was wrong. I should never have gotten mixed up with his seedy, underbelly tactics."

"I was already hung up on your past with Ethan. I was convinced you wanted to be with someone like him and were ready to dump me."

"What? Why on Earth would you think that?"

Adria rubs his neck and slouches. "Remember the night I brought in Italian food?"

"St Paolo's? Of course."

He bites his lip and then confesses, "I told you I loved you that night."

Her jaw drops. "No, you didn't. Did you?"

"I did. But you didn't hear."

"Oh my lord," she says, hiding her face in her hands. "I'm so selfish."

"No, you're not."

"I am. I was too busy consuming my thoughts with Myra." She gasps and locks eyes with him. "Too busy that I missed the beautiful boy across from me saying he loved me." She caresses his cheek. "I'm so sorry, Adrian. I don't understand how you can love me."

He grins. "It doesn't matter, because I do." He pulls her close and kisses her. "I love you so much."

"I love you more," she whispers, and then kisses him again.

As their lips pull apart, Jazz's heart swells as she watches his smile. He runs his hands through her raven hair. She never imagined she could feel this happy, especially after such a hellish night.

"See, it wasn't so bad, was it?" she asks with a smirk.

"Huh?"

"Going into a situation to pull someone out of harm."

A whisper of a laugh puffs out of him. "Oh, that."

"It could work," she says, enthusiasm bubbling inside her. "We could do this."

He rests his forehead against hers. "It could work."

She leaps backwards and bounces up and down. "Really?"

Adrian stumbles for balance. "Geez, excited much?"

She moves back to him, clutching his hands. "Adrian, I want this. I want it for us, and for the people of Maiden City. Imagine all the people we could save."

"We can't save everyone."

"Some is better than none."

His shoulders relax, and he nods. "Some is better than none."

"I've accepted I can't save everyone," she says. "I can't find Myra. I'm going to be here for her. I'll never forget her. I'll always be looking out the corner of my eye for her. But in the meantime, I can help people like Aria, who are right in front of me."

Adrian kisses her cheek. "That sounds awesome."

"I'm going to go now," Jazz says, "and explain to the people, who don't need to be here, that they should go back home."

"We can't choose who to kick out. What if we send someone packing who needs help and is too scared to ask?"

"How about this; we explain to those who seem to be here for unjust reasons, that they are to undergo a therapy session to determine what level of care they need. I guarantee the ones who need not be here, will stampede for the door."

"Sounds like a plan, but what if Ed gets overrun with therapy sessions? He was already running on empty."

"Do you think it'd be likely?"

"Will we need another therapist?"

Jazz sighs. "I already talked to Eddy about bringing another therapist onboard. We should all sit down and discuss it."

"We should. Let's work on clearing this place out."

"And we should check on Gene on the way. He texted me when we were in the car saying he had been busy. Hopefully, this place wasn't a madhouse in our absence."

They leave Adrian's room and make their way to Gene's. They open the door and are met with Tessa and Max in a romantic embrace, with their lips pressed together.

"Oh my goodness," Jazz gasps. "Sorry, didn't mean to walk in on you two."

Tessa and Max break away, their faces turning tomato red.

"Since when have you two..." Adrian begins, but awkwardly halts his sentence.

Tessa runs a hand through her pixie cut and averts her eyes. "Uh, we haven't. I mean, we just..."

"It just happened," Max says, holding back a laugh.

"I ran into Max on the way back from work," Tessa says, fidgeting in place. "We got to talking."

"Talking?" Jazz says, enjoying their bashfulness.

"She convinced me to come back," Max says, grinning at Tessa.

"*That* I'm so glad to hear," Adrian says, moving forward and patting Max's shoulder. "I'm so sorry I haven't talked to you lately."

Max sighs, shaking his head. "It's not your fault. This place was overrun."

"And that was my fault," Jazz interjects, clasping her hands in front. "I apologise. I made an error in judgement and wasn't taking care of you all first. I was thinking about my ego."

"Jazz, you already saved us by keeping the lights on and bringing in food," Tessa says. "You're a rockstar in my eyes."

Jazz giggles. "That's very kind of you to say. But I promise you guys, I'm going to be better. More attentive."

"You're cool," Max says, giving her a nod. "Tessa talked you up. We're sweet."

"I hope you two stick around a while longer," Jazz says.

Tessa and Max exchange bashful glances.

"Our cue to leave?" Adrian says to Jazz.

Jazz giggles, enjoying the awkwardness in the room.

Jazz takes Adrian by the hand and leads him down the hall. "Oh yeah. We should leave, for sure."

Free

Valeria sits on a hard blank of wood called a bed. The cement floor, walls and ceiling retain the icy temperature of the holding cell, but she hasn't shivered once. Her heart has had years of practice, strengthening her for cold places.

Through the steel bars of her cell, she watches her parents follow a guard. They stand in front of her cell, tired and desperate.

"Mother," she says dryly. "Father."

"How are you doing?" her father's voice quivers.

Valeria smirks. "Peachy."

"We will get you out of here," her mother says. "Riveras don't belong in prison."

"We want you to get the help you need," Angelo adds.

"Maybe you should have thought about that every time I asked you for a little attention," Valeria says. "Why did I have to attempt murder to get you to look at me?"

"Valeria, we aren't condoning your behaviour," her father replies.

"Really? Murder's not the next event after swimming?" Valeria says with a cackle.

"Stop being so morbid," her mother grizzles.

"Morbid?" Valeria's sarcasm lays thick on the word. "You two come down here pretending to be doting parents. You know they won't let me out. What do you think? You say a few nice words and they'll let me go free?"

"*Valeria*," her father hisses.

"This isn't the swimming pool, Pappa. You don't rule here. Geez, you don't rule anywhere."

Angelo groans. "You're an awful, hateful girl. I don't know why I bother with you."

"Because you're going to Hell, and you're trying to repent."

"Don't you dare!" Angelo yells.

"*Hell, hell, hell*," Valeria mocks.

Angelo slams his hands against the steel bars.

Valeria cackles to herself as her father curses at the bars and orders her sobbing mother to get up. She watches with glee as he snarls and demands his wife to follow him out of the room.

Her mother is a bawling mess. Losing two of her daughters in one night.

Valeria doesn't believe Aria will go back home.

She grins, happy she robbed her parents of Aria.

Serves them right.

Home

Aria slept for hours. When they arrived back at the shelter, Eddy brought a blanket and a pillow into his office so she could sleep in private.

Aria didn't let him go. He snuggled up with her, and she confirmed that not only was Valeria responsible for all her injuries, but she was also the reason for her insomnia.

Eddy reminded her she was safe now and stroked her hair. She was asleep within moments.

Aria wakes alone. She sits up, pushing the blanket down, and rubs her eyes against the protruding sunlight.

"Eddy?" her voice croaks.

She pulls herself off the couch, runs her fingers through her unruly hair, and moves to the door.

She walks into the hall, and it's empty.

Whoah.

She's never seen it empty before. And it's quiet.

"Good morning," Jazz says, greeting her warmly as she exits a room. "Did you sleep well?"

"Best sleep of my life."

"I'm so glad to hear it. And I'm so glad you're here and well. I was so scared we wouldn't see you again."

Aria smiles. "I'm here and I'm not going anywhere."

"When I worked for my father, I never made time for friends. I've been making the same mistake here. I could have connected with someone like Tessa, but I ignored her to serve my own wants. I don't want to do that again." Jazz flexes her fingers and displays a timid smile. "What I'm saying is, I hope we can be friends."

"I'd love that," Aria says. "I haven't had a friend in years."

Jazz lifts her hands and gestures to both sides of the hall. "You can have a bunch now."

"Where is everyone?" Aria asks, looking up and down the hall. "This place is usually buzzing."

Jazz's body relaxes with relief. "All the wrong people are gone. I had a grand plan to dismiss them all, but Genie worked his magic while we were out."

"What do you mean?"

"He rallied up all the volunteers and talked to the groups hanging out here. He scrutinized social media posts and studied people's background. He implied he had information to leak." Jazz smirks. "I don't condone it, but the boy moves fast."

"He's full of surprises."

"He shouldn't keep himself in a room. He needs to be out in circulation with everyone that arrives."

"He really helped me feel at home here."

"He's a bright spark, and I want him to thrive."

"Where is he? Is he with Eddy?"

"I think everyone is in the dining room," Jazz says, beckoning her to follow her. "It's nearing lunchtime."

They walk in the dining room and see the group sitting around a table. Eddy sits on the tabletop and turns as their footsteps close in.

He leaps off the table when his eyes land on Aria. "I wanted to get back to the room before you woke up. I didn't want you to wake up alone. I'm sorry."

Aria takes his hands, and he kisses her cheek. "I'm ok."

"Are you hungry?" he asks.

She pats her stomach, grinning. "Yes."

Eddy takes her hand and walks her to the table. "How's your foot?"

"It hurts, but I'll manage."

"We'll get a doctor to check it out."

"I don't want to go back to hospital."

"We'll bring the doctor here."

"Geez, you guys really can get things done," Aria says, impressed. "I'm so glad I get to be a part of this place."

"Me too," Gene says, beaming, and tapping the space beside him.

Aria sits at the table and Jazz sits opposite, next to Adrian.

"I heard you saved the day," Aria says to Gene.

Gene laughs. "It was nothing compared to what you guys went through. I just looked around the room and recognised some faces. It's not hard to scroll through social media."

"I can't believe you are walking around," Adrian says to Aria in awe. "You took a beating last night. Valeria got me once, and it knocked the air out of me."

Eddy gently rubs Aria's back. "We'll get her checked out."

"Must have been adrenaline that kept me going," Aria says, as the tenderness between her shoulder blades intensifies.

"You and Jazz are forming the kickass chick club," Gene says, bouncing in place.

"We've needed that for a long time," Adrian says, slinging an arm around Jazz.

"Absolutely," Eddy agrees.

Aria nods to Jazz, smiling. "You still need to teach me a thing or two."

Jazz smiles back. "Happy to."

After lunch, Eddy meets up with Max, and Jazz works on damage control after her blunder of a TV interview.

"D'you think Jazz can make a statement they won't twist?" Gene asks, as he, Aria and Adrian step outside into the back alley.

"She knows what not to do," Adrian replies. "She's good with words. I think she was just distracted last time."

"That happens when you're worried about impressing your parents instead of taking care of yourself," Aria says.

"Are you ok with moving out of home?" Adrian asks. "It'll be a big adjustment."

"It's a long time coming," Aria says. "I was an empty shell at home. This place might be chaotic, and I might see or hear some intense things, but here I'm alive."

"I'm so happy you're here to help," Adrian tells her, smiling.

"Oh no, oh no," Gene says, cupping a hand around his eyes and bending over as he moves behind Aria and Adrian. "Don't see me. Don't see me."

"What's wrong?" Aria asks. "Who are you hiding from?"

"That psycho girl at the end of the alley," Gene says, cowering behind her. "See? Dark glasses, blonde hair, bomber jacket. She's insane and I want nothing to do with her."

"Oh shit," Adrian says, staring up the alley.

"What?" Aria and Gene say at once.

Shock coats Adrian's face. "She's my sister."

Jazz and Aria's stories will continue in the following book...

Sneak Peek: Cara
Chapter One

Cara moves like there is a spotlight on her. Not wanting praise. Not wanting attention. More than anything, she does not want to be seen.

Always on guard, she makes decisions like every eye is watching her. This way there are no mistakes. This way no one will catch her.

The music from the DJ booth pulsates through the walls of the nightclub and jolts the floor. The neon lighting illuminates the patrons in purples and blues as they drink cocktails and grind on the dancefloor. Behind her dark tinted aviator sunglasses, Cara sees every individual perfectly. With years of training, she learnt to focus and rely on her peripheral vision. The added darkness is like a security blanket. Calmed by no one's ability to look directly into her eyes.

Cara scans the room and gauges the intoxication levels. Sometimes when her prey is too wasted, it is harder to complete the job. Their bodies flail unpredictably, and if she gets caught, they meet her with a mess of slurred and aggressive words. Something she rather not deal with.

Her eyes land on two preppy men, clinking pints of beer together. They lean against a cocktail table and throw their heads back with laughter. Cara's hands tingle with the urge to pick their pockets, as the men overtly leer at women, wanting a hook-up.

They deserve this.

She tilts her head as they provoke each other to approach another girl.

If I play the part of drunk girl, maybe they'll flash their cash on some food? It'd be good to eat something before moving on to other targets.

Cara sighs into a slump. She hates playing the drunk girl angle. It involves communicating with the creeps and letting them think they can have her. She twists her oily blonde hair over her shoulder, as she dips her dark shades slightly lower on the bridge of her nose. Her hips swing as she saunters over to them.

One guy nudges the other, a huge, cheesy grin taking up two-thirds of his face. Both men stare at Cara like a piece of meat.

Her stomach drops, but she ignores it as she scrutinises them. They wear light jackets, which will be easy to feel for anything of value in the pockets. Their tailored trousers have the signature two pockets at the front and none at the rear. The worst kind to sneak into.

Ick.

But they always let her. The fake drunk-girl-kinda-interested play is by far the easiest. It's like these guys are begging for her to do it.

"Hey there," one of them says. His dark blonde hair is slicked back and there is not a trace of stubble on his too clean face.

He's so shiny.

His friend is just as wax-looking, and pulls an arm around Cara to bring her close.

"Hey guys, what's up?" Cara says, so bubbly she can't stand it. She throws in a giggle and wants to punch herself.

Waxy guy's hand slides down her back, and Cara's insides shudder. She has learnt to mask her reactions on the outside, but is yet to master turning off inside. After years at this game, she'd hoped to deaden that part of her. Her gut will never let her. Always on guard. Trusting no one.

Cara slides a hand along his waist and taps the back of her hand against the inside of his jacket. *Mobile phone, wallet, loose cash. Easy, done.*

"Things are looking up now that you're here," Waxy says, smirking.

"What are you doing with these?" Shiny says, reaching for her glasses.

"Don't," she snaps.

They stare at her, dumbfounded.

She's quick to add a smile. "I love to add some mystery when meeting new people."

Shiny folds his arms and his smile slides left, intrigued. "Oh, mystery girl, ay. I like the sounds of that."

Cara traces a finger in a circle on Waxy's t-shirt. "You guys eating? I'm kinda down for some food."

"*Pfft.*" Waxy scoffs. "Food's no good. It doesn't let the drinks work fast enough."

"Hey, I'm down for more drinks too," Cara says, moving her arm from the inside of Waxy's coat, and leaning on Shiny. "I just want a burger too."

"Girls eating burgers is hot," Shiny says, enjoying Cara's body pressed against his.

Coins, gum packet... two mobile phones? Why does he need two?

"This place doesn't do burgers," Waxy says, somewhat agitated. Obviously pissed Cara is now leaning on his friend instead of him.

"Like *duh*," Cara says playfully. "There's the food truck out front. Let's eat, then you can buy me cocktails."

She giggles like she's had four martinis and slips her hand to Shiny's trouser pocket.

Shiny likes this a little too much for Cara's liking, and grabs her bum and squeezes hard.

Ouch, arsehole.

Her teeth grind, but she has perfected smiling over the top of it.

Shiny's face dips by hers, and he whispers with beer-stained breath, "Well, we can go outside, and ditch him in here."

"You'll get me that burger?" she whispers back.

"I'll give you all the meat you want."

Gross. He's wasting my time. I'll have to rob him because all he wants is me in an alley on my knees.

Not happening, Bucko.

Cara smiles at Shiny and slips back to Waxy. She leans into Waxy, and whispers, "And you're sure you don't wanna come?" as her hands pilfer his pockets.

His wallet slides out as her leg rubs against his. She flicks her wrist, and the wallet slides into the heavy-duty pocket of her bomber jacket. She takes the loose cash and phone. People notice the weight difference of a half-empty pocket, but not an empty one.

She works on the other pocket, leaning in closer so Shiny doesn't see her hands.

"Damn, girl, you seem like fun," Waxy says, grinning.

Cara giggles and pushes back to press against Waxy. Behind her, her hands dig in his pockets, unnoticed as the guys goofily laugh at each other.

"Will you fellas let me freshen up before we leave?"

"Do what you gotta do," Waxy says, salivating.

"I can't wait for the meat," Cara says, girlishly.

"Why wait?" Shiny whispers harshly in her ear, hands all over her bum. "We can head into the bathroom with you."

"It'll be worth the wait," Cara whispers back, sliding away.

He grabs her wrist and jerks her back.

Cara almost loses balance, but this isn't her first time in this dance. She turns her wrist over and twists his arm into a position where he's forced to let go. As soon as he does, she's quick to move. With her head down, she gets lost in the sea of purple and blue bodies that thump with the beat.

On her way, she unclips bracelets, flicks off watches, and picks pockets for loose cash.

She busts into the janitor's closet by the bar, scales the shelving, and swings herself up and through the broken window. For six months this window has been broken. For six months she has robbed the patrons. For six months, no one notices her re-offending.

The game is getting too easy.

Oof!

Cara is slammed against the brick wall of the alley. Two tattooed men with neon-coloured hair hold her back. Cara pouts as Dean approaches with a slow walk.

"Sup?" she says with a nod.

"I thought we had a deal, Girl," Dean says, dragging on a cigarette. "We are business associates, but then I find out, you're not holding up your end of the deal."

"What are you talking about?" Cara replies, playing it cool.

"For two weeks you haven't brought us clients," Dean says, blowing smoke in her direction. "How long did you intend to screw us around?"

"I'm not screwing you."

"*Dyke*," one of Dean's henchmen coughs.

Cara's eyes roll.

"I need buyers," Dean says, angling the ashy cigarette at Cara's cheek.

Cara swallows roughly. She's seen him do it before. A cigarette burn to the cheek would really make her memorable. She can't have any distinguishing marks in her line of work.

"How do you expect me to run a successful business and expand without more clients?" Dean says, angling his head so his strip of neon pink hair flaps against his shaved scalp.

"There are two guys inside," Cara says, calm and collected.

"They're gonna be pissed because I took their stuff. One had two phones, so obviously living some double life. They look like they are Province kids. Probably at university. The three phones are in my pocket."

The henchman fishes inside her jacket pockets and pulls out phones, jewellery, and cash.

"The cash is mine," Cara snaps. "You can sell the phones or use them against the dudes to get them hooked."

"We're taking everything," Dean says, dragging his cigarette again. "Consider it payment for the last two weeks."

"I haven't worked for the past two weeks," Cara pleads. She had more pressing matters than finding people for The Neons to sell drugs to. "I need the cash."

Dean instructs the henchmen to let her go, and they move down the alley with her loot.

"Not my problem, sweetheart," Dean whispers with his gravelly, nicotine-damaged voice. "You wanna survive on these streets? You play by my rules."

He walks away with another puff of his cigarette and Cara wants to clock the back of his head. She balls up her fists and internalises the anger. A good rule of thumb is, don't deck the head of a street gang. It won't end well for you.

Shit. I really wanted that damn burger.

...

Get your copy of Cara (An LGBT Cinderella Story) now!

THANK YOU FOR READING

To continue with the **Happily After When** Series, look out for the following books:

> #1 – <u>JAZZ</u>
>
> #3 – <u>CARA</u>
>
> *And many more to come!*

Other books by Emily Bourne

The **In It Together** Series:

> #1 – <u>**In A Mirror**</u>
>
> #2 – <u>**In The Haze**</u>
>
> #3 – <u>**In It Together**</u>
>
> *And many more to come*

The **Holiday Together** Short Story Collection:

> #1 – <u>**In Fiji**</u>
>
> #2 – <u>**In Chills**</u>
>
> #3 – <u>**In The Spirit**</u>

CONNECT WITH THE AUTHOR

Visit author **Emily Bourne** in the following places:

Website
www.hcpbooks.com

Newsletter
www.freebies.hcpbooks.com

Instagram
www.instagram.com/iemilybourne

9 781925 990089